T0344393

monkey secret

monkey
secret

diane glancy

TRIQUARTERLY BOOKS
NORTHWESTERN UNIVERSITY PRESS

evanston, illinois

TriQuarterly Books
Northwestern University Press
Evanston, Illinois 60208-4210

Copyright © 1995 by Diane Glancy
Published 1995 by TriQuarterly Books/Northwestern
University Press. All rights reserved. Printed in the
United States of America

ISBN 0-8101-5016-6

Library of Congress Cataloging-in-Publication Data

Glancy, Diane.
    Monkey secret / Diane Glancy.
        p.   cm.
    ISBN 0-8101-5016-6 (acid-free paper)
    1. Indians of North America—Fiction. I. Title.
    PS3557.L294M66   1995
    813'.54—dc20   95-1716
                                                        CIP

The paper used in this publication meets the minimum
requirements of the American National Standard for
Information Sciences—Permanence of Paper for
Printed Library Materials, ANSI Z.39.48-1984.

Every founder is confounded by the graven image.

JEREMIAH 10:14

CONTENTS

ACKNOWLEDGMENTS

Some of the stories in this volume were first published in the following: "Lead Horse," *Earth Song, Sky Spirit: An Anthology of Native American Writers,* edited by Clifford E. Trafzer, published 1993 by Doubleday & Company; "At the Altar of American Indian Architecture," *American Letters and Commentary*; "Minimal Indian," *Ploughshares*; "Driving to Cotter Where Harrison's Truck Broke Down," *American Institute of Discussion*; "Sketches of the Artist as a Woman," *The Mississippi Review.*

I would also like to thank Renata Treitel for reading "Monkey Secret."

monkey secret

lead horse

Rain blew through the screen. Nattie stood in the open door. Feeling the spray on her face.

A tree in the backyard slammed its door. Or maybe it was the room upstairs. The windows were still open.

Her backyard bushes beat the ground. Back and forth their fists pounded the grass.

Let the curtains stand straight out. Let the storm stomp-dance through her house. Rattle her plastic dress bags hanging on the door. Her shawl-fringe and feathers.

She watched the lid to the trash can fly across the yard like a war shield. She watched the leaves buck.

What's the battle out there, Nattie? Joes said. He scratched his ear when Nattie looked at him.

Well, he wasn't what she hoped. But it was seeing all that potential in him.

The wind wheezed through the weather stripping on the door. The whole yard shook. And it was the day of a family birthday. A relative Nattie only wanted to send a card to, usually, but now she was on her way, and the cousins were going to show up and Nattie had a sink full of dishes and a war in the yard and Joes at the table. And he was starting to hum like electricity on the backyard wire.

It's a lot for one old woman, she thought.

It'll be over soon, Joes comforted.

The relatives or the storm?

The trees raised and bowed their arms in exaggerated motions as if the cousins already pulled in the drive. But the relatives were out there under an underpass in their car. The old green Plymouth tossing a little in the gusts of wind. Chewing them but not yet swallowing. Jerking all the while with pleasure Nattie could only imagine.

She was making her corn chowder and cornbread and corn pudding. She should have said she'd meet them at Benny Bill's Ranchero. They could have a steak and dance. But the cousins didn't like that. She could outdude them any time. In fact, they couldn't dude at all. Yes. What a storm sash she was.

But Joes could still make her blush. And the cousins were coming and she was supposed to kowtow and lick their flitters. The trees swept their arms. The storm shuttered over the house like horse hooves running.

Still the rain torpedoed the house. Just like Crouper and Boaz, the cousins, when they were boys, roughhousing like monkeys upstairs, and you wanted to yell at them to stop.

You going to close that door, Nat?

When I'm ready.

She'd seen the highway once from a plane. The one time she flew. She'd felt the invisible cord that jerks a plane into the sky. A pull-toy right up to the clouds where the highway and its cloverleaf looked like cucumber pickles in a jar, the tight highway loops like curls of onions.

Maybe a spirit fell to the yard, flailing, by the looks of it. The arms and legs struggling to get up and disappear before someone could look from her house and say, hey, there's a spirit out there. The splot between the elm and oak, and the bushes beating it away. No, the wisteria didn't want any fallen spirit in their yard.

Something was being swept out of the Hunting Grounds. Maybe the Great Spirit had his war stick out.

The old hammock wind-danced.

Then Joes was at the door with her. Kissing her jaw. Rubbing his fingers across her back. Sometimes his hand went just under the fatty part of her hip.

Keep your hands on your own self, she said.

Lightning cracked so loud Nattie closed the door.

It's too late by the time you hear it, Joes told her. Closing the door's like trying to get in the canoe once the flood's started. He had his hairy hand on her stomach.

Joes, I got the cousins coming for Wilhelmina's fiftieth birthday, though I think it should be her seventieth. I'm trying to get myself geared for the smell of horehound cough drops, mentholatum and camphor.

And Fedora who was never anything but a chicken liver from the day they first sat her in the crib next to me.

Chicken livers aren't bad.

There was always some memory of the cousins knocking in Nattie's head trying to get out. But she wouldn't tell Joes. ONCE THE WORD WAS SPOKE, THE OBJECT FORMED.

In all, she was a lead horse. Not the dull silver metal, lead. But the LEED.

She remembered once when she and her former husband were returning from her mother-in-law's house in the country. Nattie was driving her mother-in-law's old car. When they finally had to take it away from her. And Nattie's husband followed her on the narrow road at night in their car. It was harder to drive out front. Yet he let her. Or rather, he waited to leave the yard so she'd be first. He was teaching her already how to get along. Teaching her already to lead.

As if she didn't know—

What's bothering you, Nattie?

I was thinking—

All of a sudden Nattie gulped. There was someone's face at the side window. Not even knocking. Not even hurrying to get in from the storm. She saw him as she turned to face Joes.

Crouper! She opened the door and jerked him in the house. The kitchen lights blinked off and on.

The other cousins stayed in the car until the wind stopped whipping the trees. The cousins got their hair piled on top their heads. They don't want the wind to bring it down, Crouper said.

Nattie could see them poking in the car out under the tree. Boaz's four-door twenty-year-old Plymouth wrapped to the ears with rain and leaves stuck to the windshield. Nothing would get through to them. Nattie'd be hearing about every storm they got caught in for years.

They held their landing-pattern for fifteen minutes.

Now tell them to hang these newspapers over their heads and get in here.

WHATEVER YOU DON'T WANT SAID, SAY IT OVER AND OVER UNTIL IT'S SO COMMON NO ONE HEARS IT ANYMORE.

That's the white man's way.

Maybe Boaz'd just turn the Plymouth around and go back to Durant, Oklahoma.

But no. How she was glad she wasn't in the car with them. Whu clumpta. Ere they cahume. The women screamed like monkeys because the wind whizzed the newspapers from their heads. But their hair was still there. Just listing a little to the side like a birch-bark canoe hanging over one ear. We brought a bag of pecans fresh out of the freezer. Fresh as if we'd just picked them up.

The four cousins: Crouper and Fedora and Boaz and Wilhelmina. Jumping up and down in the kitchen. Named with dignity and light. Why had they turned up such cocoons full of larvy? Hey! How you world travelers today? Eoouee!

Yessie. But she was the lead horse.

You need seatbelts for the run into Nattie's house. Joes whistled without knowing what he was doing. He had a lead horse by the tail. And he would ride. Yezzo.

Well, bless her up with real sunshine. But don't look like it's going to shine today.

Rain's a blessing, Wilhelmina.

I hope this isn't a token for the rest of my life.

Yes, Wilhelmina was a bumpo brain for sure.

The rainstorm sputtered over the house, seeming to let up at times—but it soon roared again.

Nattie's kitchen whummed down through her toes. As if falling from the sky. Here's the roof. Smokehole—she could say falling into it—the upstairs bedroom throw rugs. The white ceiling of the kitchen. The round table, moonlike, where she had to face her own kind. Which is the richest blessing an Indian can have. Family. She reminded herself daily. She should bead it on a deerhide bag and hang it above her stove. Maybe with a woodland tribe floral pattern.

It seemed to Nattie her house opened like a flower. The back walk, a stem. The kitchen, dining room, living room and downstairs bedroom, the wide, round petals. The upstairs room buzzing like the Great Spirit with an attack of lumbago.

Want me to close them windows upstairs? Joes asked.

No. Things need rearranged. Cleaned up.

The cousins settled in. Fedora stirring Nattie's chowder. Crouper at the kitchen table with a napkin on his lap. Boaz washing the dishes in the sink. Wilhelmina Kleenexed in the next room. Crying over her fifty years and the list of her hair.

Nattie'd hand them some quietude. Just let them stay at her house long enough.

Joes.

Whadhoney? he asked. The cousins looked at him.

She was knifing him with jamspurts. Keeping him fed. Her toes probably curled in her shoes.

A jet-fine landing. Big gawky wings stuck out like Boaz when he had dive-bombed from the dresser to the bed as a boy.

If she left Crouper alone in the house, he'd probably go through her underwear.

Come on, Wilhelmina. Get your birthday-self in here.

They sat at the table. Boaz. Fedora. Crouper. Joes. Nattie passing the cornbread and chowder. Wilhelmina dragging her wilted self to her chair. They spread in all six directions. North. South. East. West. Down. Up.

The biggest thing that happens to Fedora's when her button jar gets spilled. Crouper swallowed. Sometimes I go over and give it a nudge just so she'll have buttons to pick up.

You seem touchy, Fedora.

I thought Wilhelmina was the touchy one.

I was out yesterday morning trying to chop wood. Boaz ran the honey across his cornbread. That old dead tree's been lying across my backyard now for two years. I chopped and chopped. But it wouldn't give.

I'm not as touchy as Fedora.

Can't we just eat and be quiet? Nattie asked. Chew our cornbread. Swallow. Open our mouth and put in another bite.

A cord of wood costs more than I can afford. No sense in buying it when I got a whole dead tree in my backyard. Boaz always drank his licorice tea with loud sips. I'm going to hire someone to chop that wood.

The house rattled as they ate. Lightning bolts stroked the sky.

I knew it would rain. I heard the blackbirds talking. But they didn't say we'd be stowed-up under the underpass. Or hanging on with our teeth—

Crouper excused himself.

I've always been the youngest cousin, Wilhelmina said. I guess

I'm not used to being older. And Mother always insisted on us being nice to you, Nattie, even when you came in the house like a horse—

Boaz said, of course maybe someone from the church could come and cut that wood for me. Then I wouldn't have to pay. Your tea's always good, Nattie. Boaz took two more gulps. And your cornbread. Some of the men have chain saws. It wouldn't take them long. Better than me with the old ax. Never know how long the cold's setting in for this winter. Back in the old days we had snowstorms! We don't have them so much anymore. I remember days when I was a boy the road would be piled with snow and—

What on earth are you talking about, Boaz?

The rabbits were easy to catch because they couldn't hop in the snow. When you've seen so many winters they all stay together like buttons in the jar. Wilhelmina blew her nose.

Something hit the side of the house with a bang.

Where's Crouper? I don't want him looking in any windows around here.

Just the trash blowing around. Joes went to look.

Now if I saved my money, I could buy a chain saw. Then I'd have firewood on my backporch and I wouldn't have to worry about keeping warm, or cooking. Maybe the Handshy's boy would cut it for me. But everyone's busy. Too bad they can't say, Boaz, could I come and cut that wood for you because we just might have snow or a hard coldspell one of these days and we don't want you to be without firewood or worse that tree could fall on your house and smash it in two, or worse—

Boaz! This's my birthday, Wilhelmina said, and I say SHUDDUP!

Drag it all out, he answered—like pulling string from the drawer your mother saved until she yelled at us and we had to roll it back into a ball.

What do you want, Boaz? For us to get in the Plymouth right this minute and go cut your wood?

No, by shucks I'm just talking.

Then hang it up, Nattie said.

Empty dress bags. All of them.

No one'd ever know you carry a TOMAHAWK in your heart. Your WITCHERY sticking straight pins in that pin cushion on Fedora's wrist.

You want blood?

No coup-sticks for her. NOsirEEEooo.

If I eat Nattie's supper, Fedora'll have to let out my pants with a guessit.

Gusset, Fedora corrected.

I don't have words for the things I want to say, and the words I DO have DON'T fit the things I can say with them.

Crouper get in here!

I think people are wearing their old clothing. Not buying new. Fedora scraped the bowl of corn chowder.

Just think of all the words there are to say whatever you need to say! How I wish I knew more words. I feel sometimes there is an exact word for each tiny detail—if only I knew it. How about that ambivalent feeling when I see you, Nattie? Wilhelmina supposed. I'm delighted. Yet some remote, inexplicable dread gnaws in the back of my head.

And I want a word for the last of the afternoon just before it turns into evening.

It's called dusk, Fedora.

Not dusk. No that's too late. That's a dead afternoon. But I want the name for an old, old afternoon—full of stars just before they shine. But are geared up—

The word for after a storm when it's all wet and dripping and quiet—

The storm ain't over yet. I can still hear rain yawl against the roof, Joes said.

Let's get it out. Let's pull the string until there's none left in the drawer, Boaz said.

Then who's the man's been looking in windows around Durant? Nattie asked. He wears a sock on his head.

Maybe we should listen to the radio— Joes said.

Wilhelmina won't let us turn it on, Boaz answered. Ever since she was jilted by a radio repairman.

Crouper wears garters for his socks. I saw them on his dresser. His socks by his chair had tops so stretched he could have fit them on his head.

How do you get the tops of your socks so big?

There was a sudden rush of wind. Then momentary quiet. The sky's kinda greenish— They looked at one another. It's late in the year for tornados—

Crouper tried to excuse himself again— Thought he'd go out and keep a rightful eye on things.

Sit down, Crouper.

Fedora poked the candles into the corn pudding. Nervous as a crooked seam. Boaz sang Happy Birthday. Wilhelmina blew her nose.

The lightbulbs in the kitchen quivered again. There was a louder rush of wind. Wilhelmina screamed. Something upstairs fell over. For a moment there was a pinkish fizz of light like birthday candles. Even Boaz yelped. Nattie seemed lifted from the house. Up past the white ceiling. The throw rugs in the upstairs bedroom. The roof. Smokehole. She was Dorothy in her red moccasins. Even Toto. Barking. No that was Boaz. She was floating over Oklahoma. Above the cucumber-pickled highways and cloverleafs. Heading north. Speaking different tongues. What the dizz— Out into the great black sky. Spirits flapping like spurts of light to keep her right-side up. The cousins talking anyway—

And we know who the star is.

Wilhelmina. Our birthday girl.

What the fluck's going on? Was Nattie the only one seeing SPIRITS? Were the cousins shucking raisins into their corn pudding? Drinking coffee and licorice tea. Had someone hit her in the head with the pan of cornbread when they cleared the table? Was she just lost in a momentary daydream?

I think that was the storm's last gasp— Joes said.

I couldn't sleep otherwise, Wilhelmina commented. I have to have silence.

You could never sleep in the room with Nattie. She snores—

They all looked at Joes.

Maybe she had died. Hadn't Nattie passed a line of cars on a curve on old Highway 40 long ago? Traffic was slow and she got impatient and pulled out. The boy she was with drank too much. She was driving. And she didn't have sense to stay in line. But passed. The lead horse out there. She made it—pulling back in with an inch to spare. Why was she saved? Just making it around the cars? Maybe her own death just now caught up with her. Maybe there was someone in that oncoming car the Great Spirit didn't want dead at the moment. So she married, had a child—Drove both of them away. Nattie couldn't say what her life had meant—

No, she hadn't died. The cousins wouldn't come to see her if she wasn't there.

We're searching for truth right here with us in the universe, Nattie said.

I know what I'm doing at any given moment. It's the overall purpose of life that's evaded me, Wilhelmina said.

Right fine, Boaz commented.

Was Nattie really there in the room with her cousins?

Who can enjoy their birthday with Crouper sitting there—his face down to his ankles?

Just because we won't let him go outside.

Not without one of us going with him.

After the drive from Durant a man needs to get out and walk, Crouper insisted.

You'd walk straight to someone's back window.

What comes over you Crouper? Nattie flumed.

I dunno. I'm taking a walk and before I know it I feel someone's windowglass against my nose and they're in their house screaming that someone's at the window.

Nattie felt her hands. She wanted the cousins to be QUIET. She wanted to ask if they could see her. She had heard the HORSE HOOVES of the storm. Maybe she was still out there—over the house—She wanted her cousins to SAY SOMETHING to her so she'd know she was in her kitchen and not lifted off the migration trail of the earth. She looked at Joes and her cousins around the table. She saw she wasn't the lead horse without the others to follow. Yes. Just look at them. Head. Tail. Four Feet. It took all six. Yeow. The four known directions plus Earth and Sky. Nattie was in the SPIRIT—Boaz opened his mouth again to say something about chopping wood or—Nattie shuddered with impatience and SPOKE to her cousins. THE STORM'S A HORSE OVER US. THE WREATH OF A FLOWERING HOUSE AROUND ITS EAR. A BRAIDED MANE. ITS HOOVES TROMPING THROUGH THE YARD—LEAD HORSE OF LEAD HORSES— Yes. Nattie'd seen a SPIRIT of which they were only part.

The cousins and Joes stared at her.

Nattie'd been proud. Thinking she was the whole show. But now she'd had a VISION FROM THE SPIRIT WORLD. She'd been given the birthday gift. She'd shared it with the others.

Boaz cleared his throat with a horehound cough drop. Crouper and Fedora sat looking at one another around the kitchen table. Wilhelmina still stared at her.

Joes stood at the door. Nattie wanted to feel his hand on her stomach— She got up and went to him. The trees dripped the last of their rain into the grass.

Nothing we can't put back together, he told her. —Cept maybe the upstairs.

If a spirit had fallen in the yard, by jolly, it'd gotten up and gone on. Maybe it'd been Nattie's pride running from the HORSE.

She felt the damp curtain of the breeze on her face. She looked again to see if the cousins were still staring. But Wilhelmina was recouping. The others were starting to stir from their chairs at the kitchen table. Rising almost as children. After the spirit storm which—yes, left them touched for a moment with some pure likeness.

at the altar of american indian architecture

There's an architecture which is not shelter, but words. I say something, and a structure's there. I drive on a road close to dark. I tell a story. *Shit,* the wife may say. But I feel Cover and Meaning. I speak old Cherokee towns into memory. Keowee. Tugaloo. Chatuga.

I got something to say. I only got to find someone who'll listen.

When I stand by the road now with a flat. I repeat the old towns. Nacoochee. Nequasse. The wife wondering why the fuck she married me. My girls, Lindy and Arky, crying. The wife looking down the road to the next getting-off place like the last one. Well. What're you supposed to do? When the cordwood's stacked against you. The monkey's jumping, so to speak.

Now I pick up Liss, my new girlfriend, with her crucifix. Her fat religion. Up there on the dash of the car I'm driving with Lindy and Arky, my two daughters from different marriages, but the car's not mine, but Liss's, and not really hers, but a friend's, and her daughter's with her father for the weekend. And she has her feet on the dash. Her toenails painted red. Hanging up there by the crucifix. The underpart of her leg dancing.

"A long time ago, the earth and sky were one."

Lindy puts her Walkman in her ear.

"When the earth and sky had to separate," I say, "they cried."

"The earth and sky got divorced." Arky pulled the Walkman from her sister's ear.

"And their crying made the water they share."

Lindy nodded.

"Yes, rain's the children of the earth and sky."

"They got joint custody of the water."

I didn't say the architecture's easy. "Let me start again."

"Rain's the children they pass back and forth." I thought Lindy was listening to her Walkman, or she wanted me to think she was.

"I like it better—when it rains, the sky water-people visit the earth water-people."

"Turn up the radio," Liss, my girlfriend, says.

I reach over to pinch her.

"Stop," she slaps.

I'm riveted to my jeans she shrank when she washed them though I told her not to. We're traveling on this legbone of a road across northern Arkansas, toward the lake, where she has a cabin, or some of her friends do. Whatever the story, we have a place to go the last weekend in October. And me pulling at the crotch of my jeans past cafés and roadhouses which we'd be turning into now, except we still got a ways to go, and it's late. And my two girls are quiet in the backseat.

We're already into lake country with boats and boathouses and cabins through the trees. "The Ozarks," Liss calls it.

"The Zarks," I pinch.

Her toes dance like the last of the hard maples along the road. Up there by the dashboard altar. A crucifix with INRI under him. The blood clots like red toenails on his side.

My girls must be asleep in the backseat after complaining for what must have been most of the way because they had to leave

Halloween with their friends. We hate to wake them, but now we're hungry. Their mothers maybe fed them peanut butter sandwiches before they left is why they haven't cried to eat.

"If we stop, you think they'll sleep?"

"Lindy and Arky Abelard? Sleep?" Liss asked. "Not a chance."

We'd been taking our kids together to have something to do with them for the weekend. To fill ourselves with their words, and maybe put enough of ours in them so we wouldn't be strangers.

"Yes," I say, "his name's INRI." I pat my girl's leg. Blood clots like chilies on his side. Because I'm hungry now. But I want to make time. We didn't leave until my girlfriend's girl's father got her, and I came from work and picked up my two girls and got the architecture from their mothers, and changed at Liss's, and by that time, the sun was nearly broke.

And I'm not sure of these winding roads after dark.

"Tell us another story," the girls say when we stop.

"The monkey story?" I ask.

"The ferocious monkey story," Arky adds.

"There was a monkey named Mary Grace."

"No. That's not the story."

"Yes, it is. If I say it is."

"No, it's not."

"Give him the road. He'll get you there." Liss buries her fry in ketchup, and the girls stare at her.

"Because HENRY's on the dash," I say.

The girls laugh again, though I don't always know what's funny to them.

So I go on. "HENRY puts his hand into the brown sack, and pulls out an organ grinder. But Mary Grace won't dance. She's a MexTexArkansasOkie, and you can't make Mary mojo. Even though way down in her jeans she's doing the tune."

"You got it figured," my girl says.

"EEEeeeeeee." I do my monkey-jag.

Lindy and Arky are wild with laughter, and now I'm trying to quiet them.

I spend Saturday after breakfast with the girls. I have to watch them, who aren't used to the lake. They might walk off the dock, and I don't want them drowned. Liss sits on the porch, her feet on the rail. "I'd do the same for your daughter," I say.

I take the oarboat out. We row in the cove. I didn't get up as early in the morning as I thought. I had planned to make love to Liss, then fish same as when I was a boy, but I heard the girls before I knew it, and it was after nine. Where'd the morning go? Not even in love. I was afraid the girls would walk in on us. But it wasn't anything they haven't seen with their mothers' boyfriends staying over, Liss said.

I hadn't made love to Liss when we got to the cabin last night. I was numb after the drive in my jeans.

History is a line which sinks into the lake. Maybe to do some fishing. Maybe to say how the car spins you out as you travel. One road. Many cars. Still going through my head when I wake groggy. Traffic coming from the other way like monkeys over the Zarks.

Liss tries to turn the radio with her toes. I knock her leg. She hits back. The car nearly swerves off the road, jerking the girls in the backseat. But they're still asleep when we turn to look.

And the cars are coming toward us through the dark of the winding road, whizzing, whiz, whiz, fast as stones maybe from the shooter or the silver pellets in a pinball machine.

I don't know where the cars are coming from like a handful of leaves.

Now that the kids are curled up in the backseat we have to stop. The jeans are driving me into the sky anyway. They feel still damp in the seams. Like rawhide, they shrink as they dry.

"They'll stretch back," Liss says. "Get off it. I had a lot to do. Maybe I left them in the dryer too long. They only shrink in the length."

"Says you," I say holding the steering wheel until my hands cramp.

The leaves are about through falling, but on the road in the updraft of passing cars, they whirl around us. I like the messy roads, the cold nights, the blue-tongued smoke that rises over the cabins. Which you can't see in the dark, only smell. Lindy whines. I blew her nose at the roadhouse, and saw she still had nosebleeds. There were small blood clots on my kerchief like a cluster of red stars. Just like the whole Universe was bleeding. And Arky with a cut on her finger, Band-Aided, and me carrying them into the cabin, thinking I'm too tired to get to Liss in the sack.

Though she dozed after dinner in the car, until I woke her about which lake road to turn down.

"If I blow on you?"

"Give me till morning," I said and was probably snoring before I finished the architecture.

But she let me go.

I turned into a roadhouse for something to eat. The car lights hit the back of the trees on the other side of the narrow valley. There was a sharp drop, and the back of the restaurant overlooked the view, which at that time was black. The menu was the usual fish, burgers, and steaks. It was late, and the places were closing on the road. The waitresses were having a cigarette at a back table and the kitchen was busy washing dishes.

"What you got left?" I asked when a waitress finally came to the table.

The girls sat across from us, still dazed from sleep.

I thought the waitress looked like she had some blood. Some of the Cherokee disappeared along the trail, or ran across from Indian Territory to find something other than Oklahoma justice the Indians knew. A chance to live, mainly.

I finished the girls' burgers. Liss urged them to eat, but I didn't want them getting sick in the backseat.

I can see in the long line of oncoming cars the ancestors coming across the trail long ago from old Cherokee towns. Chota. Settico. Nobody talks about it, but in the night, they used to say the trees told the story. Even the rocks.

I could hear their voices in the noise of dishes piled in the sink. Liss was a ringer for a Cherokee too, but it turns out she says she's part Mexican. I think there's Indian blood there somewhere. But I think there's a little of it everywhere. You always see what you already are. I think anymore we're a mixing of everything. Even time's moved around.

I stopped at the phone booth and called the ancestors. I wanted to talk to them so we won't be strangers.

"Come on," Liss pleads quietly.

What do you say to someone who walked a long trail a hundred and fifty years ago? Whose feet crossed the northwest corner of Arkansas, somewhere right by the car. You can still feel them pass. You know somewhere out there now the ancestors remember the walk. In the blackest part of the sky is the origin of architecture. Since the removal of the woodland Indians. The rebuilding of cabins, barns, sheds, outhouses, smokehouses, storehouses, cellars, corncribs. Same as language. Retelling the people with all their versions of the past. I look at Henry on the dash. Even the white man's religion's got its versions. Then there's the Indian conjurers' spells to explain the next flat tire.

I call the architecture language, which is to say, story. When the large black sky rolls over at night. When the stars skid like gravel under the car. When you got so many voices hitting you, you don't know what to hear.

"Just hold on," Liss tells me, "when the stars speed by."

Where does all the darkness come from? Not the kind when the sun goes down, but the darkness in the back of the head.

"It being Halloween we dressed as white people," I told her. "It was a time we thought we could be what we wanted. The white guys chased us. They pantsed me in front of the girls."

The cruelties we carry with us like candy in our sack. Liss rocked me in her arms that night. The whole place was tight, no matter where I was.

"Get used to it, Fletch," she said.

Then I wouldn't remember it anymore.

"HENRY," I call out when the night cuts into me with blackness hard as the blade of a jacknife, and the stars scratch gravel into my back.

The ancestors crossing on the trail with their animals. The horses, oxen, dogs, soldiers, monkeys.

"Monkeys?" Arky asked.

"Well, it seems to me there were monkeys."

"You weren't there."

"I didn't have to be." I watched Liss stir the eggs.

"Walk down the road with us, Dad," Lindy says that night. Her mother didn't send anything for her to wear and Liss wraps her in a checkered tablecloth and paints her face. Arky has a dress that used to be her mother's, and a pair of heels you can't walk down the gravel road in, I say, but Arky tries. She wants some paint too. And I'm holding onto her arm, holding her up. And I'm slipping myself in the gravel. But we make it to several houses, them probably wondering who we are.

But they treat anyway. Later the girls pour their candy out on the table by the red leaves Lindy collected that afternoon. They trade what they don't like. They give me a piece for walking them, and Liss a piece for painting them.

We pass some houses in the dark, cabins, probably, the girls can go to. I'll walk with them. Lindy's mother with her foot already in her boyfriend's car when I come for her. Arky's mother angry too. For wasting time with an Indian who wasn't going anywhere, and leaving her with a daughter.

The nights I spent with the Ancestors in the sky were the ones I remember. Telling stories. It's where I learned the architecture. The structure of story over the vast openness I could fall into. My feet scraping the bed at night when I felt it coming.

I light the fireplace in the cabin. Liss spreads blankets on the two fold-down cots for the girls, and the sagging bed in the other room for us.

The way I understand it, we went out on Halloween, and HENRY unzipped our monkey suits. And we become one of the spirit beings. Walking on water. If we believe we do, you see. Didn't I see a man cross the lake yesterday? On just his feet? We got the Spirit in us now. Isn't it in church, the organ pipes fire like exhaust pipes? Yes, that's what HENRY did. Blessed our weaknesses. Rebuilt our towns. Told us new stories when our old ones erased. Yes, he's the Word, and I, Fletcher Abelard, speak the Language.

I count my blessings. A cabin for the weekend and Liss dancing before me on the braid-rug, her red toenails shiny as the blood on HENRY's side.

Sometimes when the center starts to wobble you know you're close to Truth. Because of the whiz of matter flying by. You know you're close to the moment before The Bang. When you'll Know. Like getting back to the beginning of the Universe. Up until just the second it happened. You know the Core, guessed from what you piece together. Or imagine. Maybe there's even multiple Truths for us. There's other structures to protect the Meaning.

"Just shut up," the wife would yell. "You're full of shit. Your head's nothing but air."

But I won't let Liss see.

It's my words that wear the costume. No, I wouldn't tell Liss I don't know what I'm doing. Just piecing together the multiple parts. I wouldn't let her at the face of my words for long.

There's a highway across the lake, you know. If you look at it just right. *There's old towns,* I tell her. Their campfires reflect on the dark water at night. I call out to them.

Noyoee.

Ellijoy.

Toxaway.

Chauga.

Tugeloo.

minimal indian

Now it happened in the twelfth month that James and Crowbar visited Renah, James's sister. They were there to never lift a hand. Just their fork expecting something on it.

The two men drove from Nail, Arkansas, along Highway 16 to Red Star, where Renah had her cabin nearly built into the hills. Her goats and a few hens. A woodpile. Some rusted auto parts Crowbar was thinking of asking for for his salvage yard he called Trucks and Stuff.

If he could find them under the snow.

And Renah rising early to cook, cooked until after sundown thinking already what to have the next day. Asking for nothing but a trip to the cemetery with a Christmas basket for the parents' graves. If her brother, James, and his friend, Crowbar, had made it across Highway 16 from Nail, they could give her a lift to the graveyard.

What were they doing here anyway? Expecting their Christmas fruitcake and curls of pork-rinds early?

The two men sat at the kitchen table. James stirred his coffee with fury and chopped the eggs on his plate.

Renah cleared her hands.

We open the morning with prayer.

Even before their first bite was swallowed.

EEEEEeeeee. Renah jumped on the curled edge of the linoleum floor when the Spirit moved her. She skitted across the floor in a holyghost dance. James and Crowbar just looking at her with their mouthful of eggs and toast. Even when she prayed quietly, you could hear James chewing. He might choke, you know, with a mouthful of breakfast. He had to get it down. Crowbar nudged him. But James kept chewing.

You can't hear what she says when you chew. James told him.

It was true. Crowbar tried it.

But Renah kept moving in the Spirit.

And sure enough, soon you could see the drizzling stars dry up. And soon you could see the morning coming from a long way off. Over the curls of cabin smoke. The pine trees and acorns. The morning sun round as an egg basket.

But soon James and Crowbar went back to eating. The truth of the matter was, the ceiling in Arkansas was too high for them. Somewhere up near under heaven, Renah said. They lost interest before they saw too far.

The men lived according to their own ways which were somewhat limited and shortsighted. But they could see the blue sweep of sky across the window.

James. Renah said when she'd prayed.

Whad?

I'd like to take a Christmas basket to the graves.

Id snowed, he said.

I want to go anyway.

Go f' 't. James said.

Renah hummed as she boiled rinse water for the dishes.

James had hoped Crowbar would be a brother-in-law. Renah was not an unhandsome woman, but how could he hand her to Crowbar, bible-brained as she was? She had black curls kept tight to her head. White skin. A skinny, black-haired, white-skinned woman. One of the strains of back-hill Cherokee. Whose mouth even turned up with the curve of a squirrel tail.

Crowbar owned his business, Trucks and Stuff, on the edge of Nail, Arkansas.

He had, after inventory:

2 pick-ups
or what was left of them

a backhoe

a twenty-year-old bus used by a preacher friend of Renah's

a Kenworth cab that parted from its trailer on some back curve
    with stubs of grass and dirt still hooked in the door

a rail-fence to keep out trespassers
mostly now fallen

a house with a lean-to

an assortment of
crank shafts
fenders
doors
struts
springs
shocks
engine parts

who knew what else
maybe not even Crowbar

the Trucks and Stuff sign by the road
a satellite dish
and a fifteen-year-old James McAdoo for Sheriff sign in his yard.

Politics was still the latest.

Bigger than satellite dishes.

Crowbar would be a good husband for Renah.

James didn't know why Renah never married. Maybe no one asked her. No. That wasn't true. There was Sam Jackson from Sam's Bait and Tackle over on Bull Shoals who had asked her.

And there was the traveling tool salesman.

Family meant something to Renah. She had their photos lined up on the kitchen walls and along the top of the pie safes and on lace doilies that their grandmother had tatted. Hairpin lace or something like that. The old women always had their hands going. Back and forth like a litter of birds in the trees. All chirped up all the time.

A regular backhoe at anyone who passed. Dredging up.

Renah could do it. You got the whole story from her. Whether you wanted it or not.

The only thing she cut off, when she was behind the camera, was the heads in the photos, or at least above the nose so you kind of had to guess who it was by their trousers or dress.

She was a good woman though.

After breakfast, Renah fed the hens and goats, and James and Crowbar drove Renah to the cemetery in the snow.

Renah had her Brownie camera with her.

She decided she wouldn't get out of the car, but honked James and Crowbar in the direction they should go with the Christmas basket for the parents. Since James couldn't remember. Or couldn't find the graves under the cover of snow.

Over this way.

Honk.

Now that.

Honk.

Not that way.

Honk.

Renah motioned them one way then another. Back to the left. There James.

Honk.

In the car, Renah was warm as if she'd never left her cast-iron bed in the kitchen all heaped with her string-tied rag-quilts in the darkest purples and browns and maroons.

James and Crowbar swept snow from the graves.

Renah took a photo of James and Crowbar placing the basket.

I wasn't even turned around. Crowbar said.

Won't make no difference. James answered. There'd be nothin' of us from the ears up in her picture anyway.

The car radio played Christmas music as they drove back to the road.

Then an advertisement for Burleens' hair salon.

An evangelist saying hallelujah to the snow-covered morning.

And the Singing Starbrites!

Those sisters:

Juanita
Bonita
Corita
Dorita.

Their mother spit 'em out like peas.

James waved to a car that passed. Another Cherokee. A marginal Indian to the ones powwowing and migrating and buffaloing on the plains.

The Cherokee had been a robed and turbaned tribe with curled-handled pipes, writing and reading the letters of Sequoyah's syllabary.

Full of superstitions and little-people tales, unless they'd been converted to Christianity. Even at that, they were still full of both worlds. Sometimes conjuring. Sometimes singing hymns. Not knowing anything about being an Indian.

But a somewhat farming
backyard-hung-with-quilts

canning-jar-cellared-for-a-long-winter
vegetable-patched-in-summer
few-hogged
sort of folk.

Dry goods on the shelf
a bag of material scraps in the corner

egg baskets
apple baskets
one and two pie baskets
berry baskets
potato baskets
market baskets

froes
mallets
draw-knives
string
strips of oak and willow for more baskets

bittersweet
sage
herbs hanging by the woodstove

What kind of Indian that?

Their backwoods jamming was enough to keep a regular Indian out.

James and Crowbar hadn't been converted, Renah knew. She remembered them climbing out the vestibule window of the New Covenant Church.

That's why they'd come to Red Star from Nail! The Spirit had delivered them to Renah for another chance to be saved. Hallelujah. She tossed in the seat as they drove back toward her cabin.

Especially when they came over the hills, and saw into the distance of Arkansas.

They still almost could see the smoke from the old Cherokee pipes in the winter fog rising off the ice in the streams and farm-ponds.

She told James and Crowbar how the ancestors had walked from the southeast on a forced march. Most kept going to Oklahoma. But theirs stopped here.

Except for the hand of God they wouldn't have made it.

It was a haunted land. A magical kingdom of animal transformations and mutations of borders. Too much knowledge of the old ways. When no one would talk about it. That's what they did. And a Christian God to whom they had to make a commitment. Who could come for them anytime.

There could be a revolution in Arkansas from the suppression of the old ways. Anytime. Gunshot heard nightly. Everyone digging in. Like squirrels spread-legged in the yard. Trying to uncover.

The Cherokee seemed like everyone else. Maybe another language leaping out once in a while. Little people under the house. Chimney smoke dancing on its front legs over the yard. Its hind legs in the air. But God waited for their decision. Just like everybody else.

I can see up into heaven, Renah said. Just up to God's ears. I can see his son Jesus standing by his throne, a halo bright as an egg yoke hanging over his head. A book on how to *save the lost* under his hand. I can see God's old truck parked behind his throne. I can see the long white hair that hangs to his shoulders. I just can't see his face.

James looked at Crowbar.

We'd be BLIND if we did. Renah's voice was rising again like heat from the wood stove, if they'd been in her kitchen instead of James's car. We can't stand the sight of purity. Here on earth. In these plank-floored cabins and leaning fields. The low roofs and high floors.

Yo, James said. It feels sometimes like my head is goint to meet my knees when I'm sitting at your table.

The roof leaks snow, Renah told James. If it warms up, I'll have to get the buckets, James. Otherwise I see it coming through like the joy of heaven.

Yes.

The former and latter rain often fell all day in buckets on Renah's floor. Maybe James and Crowbar could repair the leaks.

Maybe Renah could marry, and her husband could fix it.

James ate an apple from the basket as they listened to Renah.

Got another one? Crowbar asked.

The men chewed.

An apple works just like a piece of toast, James said.

It was another day under God's grace. He must be in his hip boots and fishing gear. Warming his truck in his garage. Yes God had it wrapped up. Had his inventory in line. His family photographs on the wall. His angels with their bright wings. Renah could almost see their faces, thought she could hear their wings beating like a fan belt.

EEEEEeeee.

How those Starbrites could sing:

Juanita
Bonita
Corita
Dorita.

Wuuh. Whhuuu. James and Crowbar could see their voices up there on the stage.

Around a curve in Newton County, just east of the Boston Mts., a farmer's truck loaded with chickens crossed the center line and hit James and Crowbar and Renah head-on.

There were chicken feathers and splintered chicken crates everywhere.

Renah stood up and shook herself off. Well, she was light as a feather herself. She walked down the road. Where was she going? What happened?

She saw James and Crowbar dazed in the truck.

Hens were flying up to heaven on their little wings like snow. Renah didn't know they could fly. Up over Arkansas. Past the woodcarvers in their cabins. Past hog farmers and turkey barns. The rocky soil. Logging trucks. Her goats and hens. She even saw the steam from the Dardanelle Nuclear Power Plant on Interstate 40. The dam that Renah spelled d.a.m.b. whenever she said it. That's the way you heard it around her. She wouldn't have it any other way.

And there was some sort of funny tag on her ear.

Renah even saw heaven spread out before her like hills in the distance of Arkansas. The trees were the heads of everyone who had called the name of Jesus.

And now she could see GOD.

She could see HE looked a little like Floyd Buber, her father's old friend.

She turned to tell James and Crowbar.

But they had their head caught in the fork of a tree. And the Spirit of the air wouldn't let them pass.

They suddenly looked monkey-faced, and disappeared. Renah cried out, and tried to rush after them, but she heard the angels singing.

She saw the very face of GOD. Not just ears and nose as she imaged she'd seen his body on the throne. But a whole forehead full of stars. A nose with two garages. A mouth like the opening of a backwood cave. Some sort of engineering design on his face. Well, he was a regular computer chip. She'd seen a magazine in a doctor's office once. A complicated crossroads of veins and connectives. A numbered face full of more than she could recognize at first. A whole being full of life and love.

The Starbrites had been right.

The bait date she ended with Sam Jackson when she told him of her love for GOD, and he took off the next day back to Bull Shoals.

The traveling tool salesman likewise.

But this God. And there was his son. He was the one who waited for her. He was in his old jeans down there at the end of the road where she now walked. Just like her vision had seen.

monkey secret

In the beginning God created the heaven and the
earth and the earth was without form and void.
GENESIS 1:1–2

So this is why monkeys look like people; they are
a sign of a previous human work. POPOL VUH

ONCE WE'D BEEN ABLE TO TURN INTO ANIMALS

Sometimes I'd see a paw beneath Bently's trousers, or I'd hear a growl when Stanley yawned. We all knew it. Even the cousins. But we didn't say anything about it. Except once when Harrison, my father, had been gone a while. Mother said maybe he hibernated. But he was probably with his first wife. On her grave near Haran's charch house. Maybe he burrowed into the ground. Maybe he sat over her coffin with his wings folded. A bat in a small cave formed in another age. Yes, we knew too there were ages. We were close to the last. We heard the animals at night when they didn't know we listened. They pointed to the woods out there between two stars. They'd see the ancestors blinking messages. Mother and I would hold our breath at night to hear. Out there in space, the ancestors cavorted and sang their long charch songs. EEEEEEE-

EEEEEEEEEEEE. It was a bat song we heard. Or the monkey song. I never knew when I raised my hand. If I'd see the claws.

SUNDAY SUPPER

The dining room at Bently's house on the farm was on the north, shut in winter against the biting cold with heavy drapes pulled back while we ate.

The women brought the steaming bowls to the table and called the children to their places. Bently's wife fretting about the stew getting cold in the large drafty room with its bare walls and wood floor and china cabinet that held dishes and gravy boats of Mother Pierce's.

Bently sat at the head of the table and his wife was at the foot folding napkins over bowls. "Sit down," he told her and made a short prayer before the Sunday meal. "We thank you for our benefits. Bless the meal and us, your servants. In Jesus name."

The table seated twenty with Wylie in a highchair by his mother, and several children crowded on a bench to make room for guests. But generally there were eighteen for Sunday supper: Bently Pierce, his wife and boys—Cedric, Eban, Dempster, and Wylie—and even when Cedric was gone to the university, his chair was left vacant at the table by Bently, and a plate was set for him. Then there was Harrison Pierce, my mother and me; and Stanley Pierce, his wife and children, Nathan and Nasha, my other cousins. Then there was the Pierces' hired man and his wife who helped cook and their retarded boy, Rupert; then sometimes a friend of one of the cousins; or Sister Whatley, the widow from church who had been a friend of Mother Pierce's, or the minister, Reverend Stonesifer; or someone from the church house.

Bently passed the cold meats, the chutney and fig pickles; the fried bread and bowls of vegetables and potatoes that were no longer steaming, Bently's wife regretted.

I sat by the stain on the tablecloth that looked like Jude's hoof-print dried in the mud where the gate opened into the pasture. Jude, Harrison's mule, would wait for Harrison the way I waited for food to come around the table.

Wylie in a bib frayed at the edges had already upset his fruit bowl.

"Goodness, Wylie," his mother scolded, leaning across the edge of the table to him, dabbing the juice with her napkin while he picked the pieces of fruit with his fingers and put them in his mouth.

"Use your spoon, Wylie," Bently said.

"Here, back into the bowl," Eban helped his brother.

Sister Whatley watched them, her mouth open, unconscious of herself, her old head fuzzy as the whitecaps the wind picked up on the narrow channel of the Osage by Plimsoll Bridge. She could hardly hear, but she was in the church house whenever the door opened. Her mouth receded underneath her nose, and her lower jaw jutted forward.

I thought of asking her about the woods beyond the stars. I wondered if she knew where she was going. Maybe she hadn't heard the animals. Maybe she snored through the night.

Sister Whatley's mouth would hang open as she sat near the front pew, turned at times to scratch herself and watch those around her. She was still watching Wylie, risible as she was in church when she thought of being transformed. "Glory to God," she always said.

After the meal and dessert, coffee was poured, Bently asked around the table what each had learned in Sunday school or during the week. Everyone but Mother had a turn. Even Wylie, who would giggle and hide his eyes with his hands. But Bently couldn't tolerate my mother's animal stories and little-people tales. He laid a flooring over her every time she spoke. She wouldn't have talked there anyway. But under the lake cabin and farmhouse, I heard the voices of her stories like snaps of electricity on a cold night.

Cedric gave Bently an answer that angered him once when Cedric came back from the university for Sunday supper. Bently growled and threw his butter knife on the table and broke one of Mother Pierce's dishes. Then Bently's wife was angered at Bently, and Wylie yelped, and the family went hurriedly and silently back to our farms, Stanley's wife not wanting to go to Bently's house for Sunday supper again.

HARRISON

Behind the barn Harrison stabbed the sow. The piglets watched and ate their feed. *Squeal. Squeal.* The sow said.

Death's dominion, Harrison answered as he worked.

The sow sputtered and kicked nearly out of his hands. But he jabbed her with his knee and held her down. *Jelly Shit.* He grunted at her. *Jelly Roller.*

HO TO SUMMER

"Chut!" my uncle Bently said.

The surveyors had traffic backed up from Plimsoll Bridge along the highway. The wind picked up dust from the embankment like moth's wings. "A souther," Bently called it as we waited for traffic to move. We were in the truck going from Haran, Arkansas, where we had our farms, to the lake cabin on Bull Shoals. Stanley, my other uncle, his wife, and their children would come later.

We've gone to the lake every summer since my father, Harrison, built the cabin on our hill and the dock and boat-shed down the hill on the lake, where he made the one, the nine, the four, and the eight, when he was through, which was the years time was when he had finished.

In the winter we lived near Haran on the land that had been my grandpa Father Pierce's. But that land had been tamed and divided into three farms when Father Pierce died. And looking for another wilderness to settle, they bought the point above the Osage even before the river was dammed.

There were three Pierce brothers: Bently, Harrison, and Stanley. Bently had the four boys, Stanley was Nate and Nasha's father, and Harrison, mine. Harrison was the oldest. He'd married a woman who was barren for fifteen years, then died in childbirth. I was the only child of his second wife, the daughter of Harrison's old age.

The wind through the rock hills of northern Arkansas shook the truck. Eban and Dempster, two of Bently's boys who were my cousins, and I looked toward the bridge that was being widened, until the blowing sanddust made us hide our eyes.

"A harper!" Bently said. "Stanley's chirruping at the farm." He hit his knee and guffawed as they sat in the cab of the truck; Bently's wife holding Wylie. Even Harrison laughed. Stanley was the inventor of anemometers, wind gauges, had them on his house and barn, his shed and fences. One was a sock tied to a pole. Bently always said that Stanley was born in a windstorm. Bently got out of the truck and the wind took his hat in a gust over the edge of the highway into a ravine. His arm jerked toward it, but he let it go, already too far ahead down toward the river.

"If you unfold that tarp," Bently yelled to us, "hold on to it. The wind will carry it back to Haran." He was going to talk to the surveyors, but turned before he went. "I'll unfold it for you," he said.

Bently climbed into the truck bed and tied the tarp to the corners of the truck as we held the edges for him. "Now we won't lose anything," Bently said to us. "You can quit fretting."

"We were shivering anyway," Dempster told his father. The wind was cold as we got toward the lake, and whistled through the rock bluffs and wooded hills of the low gorges.

Bently, Argus of the surveyors, held to his coat and walked up the road. Eban, Dempster, and I settled among the chairs and bed-ding, my wooden chest and the boxes of Mason jars and Bently's books they were taking to the lake. I held to Nicodemus, the stuffed toy owl that Cedric, Bently's oldest boy, had given me. I listened to Eban talk about the goat that Stanley was waiting for at the farm. Stanley was the only Pierce who still farmed steadily. Harrison had retired and Bently, who had sold his field to Stanley, taught school. The tarp flopped over us and we huddled together in the dark. I felt the truck move slowly, then halt again.

Harrison had wrapped his first wife in the linsey-woolsey the night she died and carried her down the road with her child not born. The Christian women prayed, but their prayers ascended into the night. The wagon creaking on its wheels crossed the creek at high water, and Harrison saw his first wife pass away.

Getting born is hard, Bently said later. The ankle, fist and thigh that wouldn't come. He'd seen the white clouds across her face, the last flicker of consciousness, the hands that clutched her shawl where the pain had been. Harrison sobbed at her bed.

She's the lily of the valley
the haze on early fields—

The minister, Reverend Stonesifer, commended her soul unto God and looked for the resurrection on the last day. The family stayed in the cemetery until the last clod of dirt was in the ground. Then Harrison plowed his creekbottom pasture into night, woke at 4:30, talked to her on the edge of the sun until the haze lifted and plowed his pasture back into night.

My mother and I, never speaking, weeded the new tomatoes and onions in the garden and sat on the porch of our farmhouse on Kingdom Road near Haran while Harrison was in the creek-bottoms. I hungered for words, the way Harrison hungered for his first wife.

Traffic began to move. Bently got into the truck when we crossed Plimsoll Bridge and I thought that water running into the lake would be at our cabin before I would. I held Nicodemus. From under a corner of the tarp, I watched behind us where the road went away faster.

SALMER'S LANDING

"In the beginning of the territory," one of the old men said, "I was making trails into the wilderness when I discovered the lake."

The others just listened and chewed. They'd shake their head as if yes wasn't it true, or they'd sit thinking if the story was better than their own.

The old men at Salmer's Landing were backwoodsmen. I listened to their stories while Harrison went up to the store for groceries.

"Harrison said that Bull Shoals was made by a dam on the Osage River," I told him.

"He did, did he, Jean," the old man said.

"And not so very long either."

The others slapped their knees and laughed that you couldn't put one over on her, while I shooed away Salmer's dog and the little bugs flying around him.

Then Harrison came down from the store.

"Yes '33 it was," the old man said and I'd wave to them from the boat as we left.

THE WOODEN TUB

"Eban!" I called to my cousin, who was fishing along the cove. "I found the oars in the boat-shed." He shaded his eyes and I yelled again that the oars were under the canvas and he waved his arm. They'd been lost since last summer and I was glad I'd found them.

I pulled the oars outside and went back into the boat-shed. We've had the *Commodore* as long as I could remember. If she wasn't the oldest rowboat on the lake she looked like it. The green paint on her wooden boards had peeled into the red underneath. My father gave it to me and Nathan and Eban one summer. He said it was time the three of us had a wooden tub. It was ours anyway, long before he said we could have it.

I moved a stepladder to get into a corner and saw the ladder had fallen on the minnow bucket. I was trying to straighten it when I heard a car. It was too soon for Bently to be back from the backwoods school he had started, so I thought it must be Stanley unless someone was lost because we had the last cabin on the lake road. I looked out of the boat-shed and the cloud of dust from the road was already to the first big tree. I started up the hill and Eban ran after me.

When we got to the top of the hill, Stanley's station wagon was turning into the clearing. Nate and Nasha got out of the car and we went back down the hill. Stanley didn't come to the lake often, not trusting the Pierces' hired man with our field and gardens.

"Where's Cedric?" I asked, who was Bently's oldest boy, because he was supposed to be with them.

"We got a letter and he won't be back yet," Nathan said about our cousin.

Cedric went to a university in Missouri, after he got over his fever, and I guess he had to stay there, even in the summer. Eban said that he was glad. Cedric always walked off down the lake road by himself and didn't come back for a long while. I asked him once where he went. To his cove, he said, and walked away. I still don't know where it is but I'm going to find it. The *Commodore* would take us there.

"The *Commodore* is floating," Nasha said when we got down to the dock.

"Jean and I got her out of dry dock before you came," Eban said, and got in to show Nate and Nasha that the *Commodore* would float with someone in it.

"Have you had her out?"

"We've left her tied to the dock all week," Eban answered, pushing the dark hair from his face.

"Otherwise she'd sink," I said. The *Commodore*'s boards shrink during the winter and when we take her out of the boat-shed for the summer, it is a while before the old wooden rowboat will float. Eban and I had gone down to the dock every morning with our tin cans to bail water until the boards swelled. Then she was good until fall.

Nathan threw a life jacket to Nasha and Eban. I carried the other jacket to the boat while Eban ran up the hill to ask his mother if he could go. Nathan got the oars that I found. I saw the beads of sweat on his face.

Eban's mother said that he couldn't go far and I said not even out of the cove when he got into the boat.

"No," he answered and gave us an apple that Stanley's wife had given him for us. But Eban didn't make any difference because we were barely away from the dock when he and Nathan thought they saw Eban's fishing pole. It had fallen off a rock and they thought he caught a fish, so they rowed to the side of the cove.

I got out of the *Commodore* and walked back to the boat-shed with Nasha. I couldn't bend the minnow bucket back into shape, so I filled it with sand on the beach and buried my apple core in it.

I heard Nathan, Eban, and Dempster on the dock in the morning. I listened to the lake for a while and watched the leaves from my window. The cabin was built on a hill and the leaves of the shorter trees were at the window because I slept in a back corner of the cabin which was lifted off the downside of the hill with stilts. I could hear the boats on the lake, but they were far away and the morning was quiet enough that I could almost hear Salmer's dog bark at the landing. I started to go back to sleep, but Nicodemus had fallen on the floor and when I reached down to get him I was awake.

"I thought you were going to sleep all day," Eban said when I got down to the dock.

"I guess you've rowed around the whole lake." I saw that Eban wore his captain's hat.

I carried the life jackets to the *Commodore* because Harrison had said we could go out of our cove, and Eban ran up the hill to ask his mother if he could go. Nathan went into the boat-shed and found the hammer that Eban had been looking for. He was nailing the board when Eban came panting back down the hill and said that he could go.

Nathan looked the *Commodore* over. "That board should hold," he said, giving the hammer to Dempster to take back to the boat-shed. The warped seat had come loose from the side of the boat.

But Dempster protested, sensing that he was going to be left behind. Wylie also cried from the top of the hill where his mother tied him to the tree beside the cabin with a long rope. Wylie had wandered off the dock once and almost drowned.

Nasha decided that she would stay with Dempster. "You're too little to go," she told her cousin and he wailed.

I got into the bow of the *Commodore* and Nathan untied the boat and I pushed it away from the dock when Eban was in, but I didn't push hard enough and Nate had to use his oar.

"I wish Cedric were here," I said after Eban told me about the fish he had caught. "But his cove is around here somewhere." I turned to see if they were looking at me. "And I bet there are a lot of fish in it." Eban was hitting a twig with his oar. "Is that what he does there, Eban?"

"Does where?"

"In his cove, the place he always goes."

"He just goes there," he said, rowing again, and I pulled on my oar at the same time.

I could still hear Wylie and Dempster howling. "Oh," I said.

Nate said, "He doesn't take a fishing pole."

"Maybe he has one he keeps there," I said. "Do you think so, Ebe?"

"I don't know." He pushed his captain's hat back with his thumb. "He always goes alone."

"He's gone long enough to fish," Nathan said.

"I bet it's around Salmer's Landing because I see him walking up that way."

"The lake road goes along the top of the hill," Nate said, looking up at the ridge from the water.

"Nasha and I get tired of the same places," I said, "always the same coves."

"We could follow it and not get lost."

"My mother doesn't like for me to go very far." I told Eban that we could always see the tall trees by our cabin. East of our cove was the main channel of water, and the three tall trees could be seen from across the lake, but Harrison wouldn't let us go that way. To the west, the shore formed other coves along the bottom of the hill. There were a couple of coves before Salmer's Landing, but we had discovered them in other summers, so we kept rowing.

"How would you know if we did find it?" Eban asked.

"I would just know, Eban," I answered, "and will you sit up straight?" It had been my turn to row with Nathan for a while, and Eban in the bow was leaning on the starboard side of the *Commodore* which made the old boat hard to row. "Trade places with me, Eban." I was getting tired and the boat kept turning sideways because I couldn't keep up with Nathan.

"Jean can't row the boat—"

"Jean's a girl," Nathan said.

"Eban gets tired too," I said.

Even Nathan was tired of rowing and we stopped at Salmer's

Landing to listen to the stories the old men told. I thought about asking them if they knew where Cedric's cove was, but I didn't think they would. Cedric's cove didn't change. When the old backwoodsmen finished their stories, I got in the bow of the *Commodore* before Eban could, since I was a girl. And they pushed off from the dock.

"Let's try this cove," Nathan said when we were around the next bend.

Eban said, "That's not the way."

"How do you know?"

"Cedric is my brother."

"Did he tell you where it is, did he?"

"No," Eban said.

"You and Jean think—"

"Keep rowing, Nate," I said. We were near the rocks along the shore and I was afraid we would bump against them. But Nathan and Eban kept arguing and I rocked with the *Commodore*, wherever she was going. A water bug raced with the *Commodore*. It was going faster than the *Commodore* almost but the *Commodore* would win. It would not. It would too. A piece of driftwood got in the waterbug's way and he had to turn another way. *Lost* said the waterbug.

"We are not." I heard Nathan say. "The road is right there, we just can't see it."

Eban looked up the hill where Nathan pointed and then he turned around.

"The trees are still there," I said, looking around too, shading my eyes, for the sun was straight above us.

"I wish Cedric were here," Eban said.

"Well he isn't," Nathan answered.

"Then I wish we had stayed in our cove and painted the *Commodore*."

"It would have taken days for the wood to dry and days for you to paint the boat and you would have wanted to go for a ride before that," I was shouting at them when the *Commodore* thumped into a log and I fell back and hit my head on the bow. I sat back up to see what had happened. "And if you would watch where you're going you wouldn't bump into logs," I yelled at them.

But Nathan saw a large fish swim away from the log and he didn't hear me. "A crappie!" He yelled to Eban and they leaned over the side of the boat to see where the fish had gone and the port side of the *Commodore* went under water. We sat up fast in the boat but water kept coming in and coming in and then the water stopped. She was on the bottom.

My feet were still in the *Commodore* but my life jacket held me off the bow and then I was no longer afraid.

We got out of the boat and Eban waded to the shore. Nathan and I pushed the log away. It was an old log with moss covering it that had been in the water a long time. We tried to drag the *Commodore* along the bottom to the shore.

"This is like a barge," I said. "A big, waterlogged barge!"

"Come and help us, Eban," Nate said. But Eban was walking around the shore with his captain's hat pushed back on his head.

"Barge!"

Now Eban had his mouth open trying to lick some gnats that flew around us. I could hear the water squish in his red shoes.

"Barge!"

"It's your fault we're here," Eban said to me. Nathan laughed. "Maybe this is Cedric's—"

"Shut up!"

Maybe Cedric's cove was around the next bend and if it wasn't there, I thought, it would be around the next bend or the next and I was going to find it. Eban was going to stay in our cove with Dempster and Wylie. Maybe Nathan, even Nasha, could come.

"Nathan," I asked. "What happens to these leaves in the winter?" Harrison was boarding up the windows of the cabin.

"They fall."

"But where do they go?" I asked because there weren't enough old leaves on the ground.

"They crumble into dust and are lost in the dirt."

"No," Eban said. "The wind blows them away."

"Where does it blow them?" I asked.

"Just away, someplace," he answered. "There's a place they go."

"Jean," Nathan said suddenly. "I've been calling you, can't you hear?"

"Yes." I answered looking up at him.

"What are you doing in the stupid dirt anyway?"

"It's not stupid," I said.

"Eban and I are going down the lake road. Want to come?" I jumped up and told him that I did.

"Harrison said we had to take you and Nasha."

"Where are we going?" I asked when I was behind them on the road.

"Someplace," Eban answered without looking around.

"As far away as the apple orchard?" I asked because it was as far away as I could think of.

"Maybe," they said.

"Probably not," I said. It was getting late and besides, they always left the lake road and went down the hill to the lake before we got very far. Nasha and I followed them down the road in the low sun that flickered through the trees.

When we got to Salmer's Landing they turned down the wooden steps like I knew they would.

"We're looking for a cove," Eban interrupted.

"We got plenty of 'em around 'ere." One of the backwoods-men chawed.

"It's a cove for Jean," Nathan said. "One like Cedric's."

I glared at Nathan and Eban.

"Old Rackensack was part of the Louisiana Purchase." The old men continued their conversation. "Were a state in 1819."

"Naw. 1836. It weren't but territory in '19."

Jarley hit his knee. He'd been outdone again. "Any-wise," he said as though it didn't matter what they said, "my ancestors was eating fatback and turnip green in these hills 'fore Arkansas were even territory."

"Haw!" Another backwoodsman said.

"What do yeu want with yeur cove?" they asked me.

"I just want a place to go."

A boat came into the landing and we tossed on the dock in the waves.

"Which cove do yeu want?" Jarley spit his tobacco into the lake while the man filled his boat tank with gasoline and the woman went up to Salmer's store with the horseshoe over the door.

"I won't know until I find it."

He shook his head that he understood.

"Quite a job your Bently did, *he he,*" the backwoodsman laughed. "Gets the school teacher riled and takes the schoolhouse in't summer." He nudged the arm of the man sitting by him.

"Never did take to him neither," the other one said.

The backwoodsman who couldn't hear smiled like we were talking about him.

"Only Bently Pierce could strike lightnin' harder than 'im. The Pierces will rule Arkansas."

"The n'uther they will, by thunder," the last one said.

The dock was funked with gasoline and exhaust fumes and I told Nathan and Eban that I was leaving as the old men talked. They soon followed me. The backwoodsman who was hard-of-hearing tipped his hat as we left.

"Will the Pierces rule Arkansas?" Eban asked.

"Of course not," I said.

A car passed on the lake road and we hid our faces from the dust that flew behind it. Gravel had scattered under the car, making a pecking sound. I thought at first that it might be Bently returning from the schoolhouse and I could ride back to the cabin, but it wasn't Bently who passed.

When the dust cleared, we started down the road toward our cabins. All around us the sun poked into the hills of Arkansas like the shining wheel to Stanley's airplane he thought he could build. And caught in that weave of dusk, the gray and yellow dress I wore across the sky, sash flying in the wind, searching clouds and leaves for the wheel gone down in the wool pocket of the night.

THE CHARCH HOUSE

The starps of the white charch house near Haran, the grove of fir trees, the cemetery stones like rats' heads. Muther held my hand. Harrison was at his furst wife's stone, talking to her, taking her a flar.

Dempster meanwhile crawled under the church. The corners sat on rocks to hold it off the ground like the ark afloat in 'ar. Bently, mad as a wild hog, called Dempster back.

I will abide in thy tabernacle foreber. I will trust in the covert of thy wings. Sister Whatley churped on the starps.

But Dempster was gone. Changed into a sloth or badger or a whip-tailed lizard. We heard him scratching in the leaves under

the charch. Eban said he heard him eating walnuts. Nasha said
she'd seen him eating field grass.

THE SERMON

"There were dark and terrible things in our history," Reverend
Stonesifer said inside the charch house.

"Te Deum," Bently answered loudly.

*The dark and terrible things were also in our hearts. We weren't
to look. No we weren't. But just go on living on our farms—and
lakes if we had to. As if tilling the ground which was the duty the
Living Lord God had given us wasn't enough. And we had to aug-
ment it and go off to a lake but even there Reverend Stonesifer said
he knew we went to charch. And there was nothing to do anyway to
change the Pierce brothers we all knew how stubborn they were.*

Sister Whatley turned from the front row and looked at us.
"Glory to God," she said. I watched her fuzzed white hair as she
stared. And Rupert, the hired man's retarded boy, stuck in one of
Reverend Stonesifer's dark places, started to howl like he did
sometimes on the farm, but the hired man's wife clapped her
hand quickly to his head.

*Yes we made our lake cabins and boat-sheds and docks and only
the Living Lord God knew what else we did but we weren't to judge
our brothers no we weren't no matter how full of sin. We were just
supposed to live and make our living from the land and don't marry
our cousins and whatever else* Reverend Stonesifer thought up to
say in the charch house while Harrison sat on the edge of the pew
and Mother was quiet and far away in herself and Bently and his
wife kept their boys from wiggling and Nathan and Nasha sat quietly and sometimes yawned between Stanley and his wife.

*There was no escape from what we were. We were bound on this
earth until we died.* I held Cedric's hand when he was in church,

but now when Cedric was gone, I sat between Harrison and Bently and heard their stomachs growl. I saw the legs of Eban and Dempster between Bently and his wife. Sometimes I watched Wylie struggling in his mother's arms, his legs digging like some animal trying to work its way out of the ground.

CEDRIC'S COVE

"What have you been doing?" Cedric asked on the shore.

I was passing the stony beach to walk up the hill. I looked down and didn't answer for a minute. I had to think of one.

"Nothing," I said.

"Did you ever find my cove?"

I looked at Cedric because I thought he would be smiling but he just wanted to know.

"Didn't Eban tell you that we sank the *Commodore*?"

"I mean by yourself—after that."

"No." And I asked Cedric where he had been for so long because he didn't come until the beginning of August and not at all last summer. He hadn't even been back to Haran.

I had seen him on the beach but I hadn't talked to him. I walked up the hill when Cedric started reading again. I covered my feet in the dust and dug in the dirt under my swing with a twig until my mother called me in to take a bath.

I was a rhinoceros on the bank of a river in the great wilderness eating moss from the logs that floated past. Chew. And I was finding the great discoveries in the great wilderness. I sat on the river bank and dried in the sun. Chew. Chew. Take me with you said the hunters, to where you go. And I went under the water of the river in the great wilderness undiscovered by the great discoverers.

I was sitting in my swing when Cedric came out of his cabin and walked toward the lake road.

"Take me with you," I called and he held out his hand.

"Jean," I heard my mother when I got to the lake road.

"What?" I answered.

"What did you do to the sponge?"

"The bath sponge?"

"Yes, Jean."

"I chewed it," I said and ran after Cedric. "Where are you going?" I asked.

"To my cove," he said.

When we passed Salmer's Landing I wanted to yell to the old men that I was going to Cedric's cove, but I didn't.

"Is it far, Cedric?"

"Yes," he answered.

Maybe in the woods he had a place, I thought, but a cove, he always said. I found a small branch and pulled it along behind us.

"Does your fever ever come back?"

"No."

We passed the cove that Nate, Eban, and I had been in last summer when the *Commodore* filled with water and we had to climb the hill and walk home, and Harrison had to come and get the *Commodore* the next day with his boat. We painted the *Commodore* as soon as it dried out because the *Commodore* was in the boat-shed for almost the rest of the summer and when Harrison finally put it back in the water we couldn't go beyond Salmer's Landing.

"Cedric."

"What?"

"Are you really going to your cove?"

"Yes."

I held his hand when I passed the woods where other back-woodsmen lived. They broke into our cabin once when we were gone and Bently warned us about that part of the road. Going into the woods was like *snaking*—lifting the ramp to Bently's shed. More often than not there'd be a black snake and I would run for Bently and he'd come with the hoe and beat it fiercely to death. Then Dempster or Eban would tell Stanley, who wanted Bently to leave the snakes alone.

I let Cedric's hand go as we passed some cabins that were being built on the lake road. After a while I grew tired of walking. But I followed Cedric all the way down our long lake road until we came to the apple orchard near the highway, where he turned off the road into the woody ravine and I left the branch I had pulled.

I took his hand again until we climbed the far side of the ravine that went into the orchard. Then we walked down through the orchard until we were almost to the water.

The apple orchard was on a slope between the lake road and the lake. The land leveled off from the point at the end of the lake road where we had our cabins, and there was not a steep hill down to the lake like there was at our place.

"Let's rest a while," Cedric said sitting down under a tree.

"And then we'll go to your cove?" I asked.

"Yes," he answered and I sat down under the tree with him and started to pull the grass.

"Do you still have Nicodemus?" he asked.

"Yes."

"I haven't seen him."

"I keep him in my wooden chest."

"What else do you keep in the chest?"

"I don't know, Cedric," I said. "It changes. I used to bring my things to the lake in it." I looked around the orchard again because I hadn't been farther than the stand on the road where they sold apples. "Is your cove far from here?"

"No. Tell me about the chest. I haven't seen it in a while either," he said.

"Harrison went to Georgia to meet Stanley after the war and he met a wood-carver who made the chest. The wood for my chest came from a swamp in Georgia and it's gnarled," I said, trying to put back the grass I'd pulled. "And he carved a fruit on the sides of the chest that are not apples, Cedric, but *pomegranates*."

"Where did he find pomegranates in Georgia?"

"He carved the chest for me, Cedric, they didn't have to be there."

"But they're not here either," he shrugged at the orchard.

"That doesn't make any difference," I said, "he could have thought they were. Do you see?"

He smiled.

"I wonder why he did carve pomegranates." I asked presently looking through the straight rows of the orchard.

"You ought to know, Jean," Cedric said to me. "You're trying to do the same thing."

"Are you saying I copy?"

"That's not what I meant, Jean," Cedric said. "Why would he think pomegranates were here?"

"Because he thought, Cedric—" I paused. "I asked you that question."

"But I think you can answer it."

"Cedric. If the wood-carver were here with us now, if we brought him here and didn't tell him where he was, do you think he'd know?"

"I think you can answer that too," Cedric said.

CANNING

The light always turned blue just before sundown on the edge of Haran, Arkansas. The yellowed wallpaper in our kitchen looked green. The leaves on the wallpaper bloomed again.

I watched the hired man's wife in the kitchen. Her mouth packed full of teeth. She shrieked out the door to her husband. Rupert, their boy, was somewhere in the barn. All out everywhere since Rupert hanged his dog.

The kitchen just about half clapboard. The pots and kettles all noisy afloat like rowboats on the lake. The piles of papers. Peelings. Stems. Seeds. Lids. Knives. Glass jars. Rubber canning rings.

Steam cumbered the room. Bently's wife clittered at the table. The wuzzards and hemen. The brushfires on the stove.

The backdoor praizen the land. The little people running out the door from the corner of my eye like white flashes of light. Like white seeds thrown out from someone's hand.

Bently would be out there again all night. Blowing his horn. All wind up to keep the wild hogs from our harvest. The jet light in the door now dark.

Cedric held me in the backyard dark. One by one my cousins walked off while Cedric talked. I heard Rupert howling in the barn. Get up. Cedric said. Gidyup. I laughed. Cedric told his stories. Bounced me on him. Like riding a mule Cedric I told.

Sister Whatley died just as Bently's wife put up her last canning jar on the shelf. "Ged widden." She said as if we knew what she meant.

The women piled the church table full of food. Potatoes. Cured ham. Sumac tea. Green tomato pie. Fig pickles. Chutney. Turnips. Green beans.

Reverend Stonesifer lifted his arms to the heaven Whatley sat in now. She was up there eating at the long table stretched out before the Lord. The angels swatting the flies away. She was reaping her pleasure now. Yes. She was with him there. Whatley knew what Reverend Stonesifer and the rest of us yet had to find. She knew the terrible secret of our lives now that she was far enough away she couldn't tell.

MONKEY SECRET

"Wagontracks into the woods." Nathan pointed and hit the ditchweeds with his stick.

"Let's follow them," Eban said with his foot on the rickety fence that stood between the road and the lake woods.

"We're not supposed to go into the woods," Nasha told them.

"Who said?" Eban asked.

"We're not supposed to."

Nathan and Eban looked at me and Nathan leaned under the fence and we followed him into the woods on the side of the lake road away from the lake. Already cockleburs stuck to my socks. Bently's wife would fuss when she picked them out.

Eban pushed ahead of Nathan and led the way on the overgrown wagontracks that went back into the woods.

"Don't be afraid," he told us.

"Come on, Nasha," I called when she trailed behind. The branches swept against me and I told Nathan to stop letting them fling back. We passed clearings as well as narrow places where the thickets had closed in on the tracks.

There was a great secret in the woods. Possibly Cedric knew. No one spoke of it. But sometimes at night when they talked on the porches of the cabins, I would hear Bently tell the Indian story and his wife would hush him. But he would still talk until the voices sounded like they were underwater, and I knew I was falling asleep though I tried not to.

"I want to go back to the road," Nasha said.

"Go ahead then," Eban called. "We're going to push through."

"Slow up," I interrupted Eban as he trailblazed for us.

"I don't like the woods," Nasha remarked.

"I don't either."

A butterfly flitted its wings on the trail before us.

"A viceroy," Eban stopped. Bently had given him an insect book and Eban thought he knew everything.

I watched the eyes on its wings. It stayed there in the wagontracks opening and closing its wings for us to see. For us to look at its brown silk wings with eyes on them. For us to know it was lovelier than we ever would be. Unless maybe it would be in the hereafter, Reverend Stonesifer would say. Maybe it was Sister Whatley transformed and migrating between Haran and the lake to tell us what we needed to know. Maybe it was the child of Harrison's first wife, saying it was finally born.

But sometimes when I looked at the butterfly, I saw a frog head. Then a bird's head with a beak and eye from the side when I looked again. All things coming and going together.

It was like a ghost voice you could hear across the lake. One time, you know, when the lake was first dammed, bodies came out of the graves. They thought they had moved most of the cemetery, but there were bodies no one knew were there, and they came out of the ground when the cemetery went underwater. And they rose to the surface and floated in the water for us to look at and wonder how a person got to be that way.

That was it. The butterflies were flagmen waving the spirits over when we came along the road. And in the end, they were probably waving us away too so we wouldn't go too far.

"What do you think is ahead?" Nathan asked.

"I don't know." Eban answered. "The wagon tracks have been here a long time." Eban stood on a tree stump.

"What do you see?"

"Nothing but the woods."

"How far are we going?" Nathan asked following Eban.

"To the end of the tracks."

"He's looking for the place the leaves go," Nasha turned to me.

We walked through the woods until we came to a clearing. I felt Eban stiffen.

"What is it?"

We looked through the trees to a clearing where there was a tree with a growth at the bottom that looked like a monkey with its arms crossed over its knees. The sun was shining straight on it. Somehow the stream of light got through the trees. I expected the monkey to turn to us and speak.

"What if he was a person once?" Nathan asked.

"It's why the animals don't talk." I felt him shiver. "They would be able to tell us what we can't know."

"What?"

"I don't know."

"Let's go back to the lake road," Nasha begged.

"The monkeys are the remains of a kingdom that was once in Arkansas." Eban told us as we backed away from the tree.

"Har." Nathan said. "They aren't nowhere but in the zoo at Little Rock."

"We used our brain to think up bad ways of doing things." Nasha agreed.

"That's why you're pea-brained," Eban said to Nathan as we walked through the woods. "So you can't get into trouble."

"But we still do," I answered.

I remembered when Rupert had come with us to the lake once. We called him into the woods to pick some leaves for us. He was supposed to mash them for our food. We watched him pick them. We said we couldn't help him. We had other things to do. We divided the work on the trail. That's how we survived.

His eyes swelled shut and the country doctor wasn't sure it was poison ivy. He'd never seen anyone with it so bad. Rupert soaked in a cold tub in the yard and we sat under the cabin listening to his howls.

All night the locust. Cicada. Bird sounds. The wild bugs hummed with the monkey-secret trying to get through.

It came back inside my head. The rain falling straight down against the dark trees. The fretful thunder above us. Ghosts of the old explosion that diffused us. Made us small. We got in trouble knowing too much. But sometimes we heard the echo of the tremendous fall of gorge and ravine all raking together like the first dam on the Osage river which rose a foot every twelve hours. The water held back swirling up the hills, wanting out, knowing it was trapped, pulling bodies out of unmarked graves to claw the bars of its cage.

Somewhere in a dream I heard Sister Whatley speaking from heaven. Saying *go back. Go back.*

In the morning, rain on the vent of the cabin sounded like a car on the gravel road. The spirits were going somewhere. The bucket of water was dancing on the porch. The rain sweeping over the lake. The first wheel going and going again when I got away from everyone. From all the talking. And listened.

The rain was so raucous because it had come so far and heaven was a noisy place. It could drown the fish that swam on the shore-edge. The rain was loud because it had been in heaven where God roared down the hall and threw his drinking cup over the smallest thing. He rolled his meat-cart with iron wheels and the rain alone had escaped to tell.

THE LITTLE PEOPLE

"The little people's been here." Mother said when we came into the farmhouse after the lake. Something had moved, or there was a mess somewhere. Usually a pile of her spilled tobacco.

"It's just a nest of mice in the mattress," Harrison would say. But Mother knew it was the little people.

They were mischievous. They were supposed to mess things up so they really didn't do anything wrong. Wylie had seen them. Sometimes he talked about the time he nearly drowned until Bently's wife yelled at him to be quiet. *He'd seen them,* he said. An underwater tribe. Little people and backwoods folks full of air bubble words.

"Maybe even the lost monkey kingdom of Arkansas," Dempster said and Bently's wife yelled at both of them.

I worked with my words at night by the kerosene lamp on the kitchen table. Tearing them up. Splitting them and pasting their parts together until they sounded like the backwoods talk I heard and couldn't understand. Like my mother's Indian people she told me about when Harrison was hunting or in the creekbottoms. I'd hear the old language. I'd see the spirits in the corner of the room at night. They were shy and didn't want us to look at them. We'd sit around the table. Mother would lick the back of her hands. Sometimes they'd come and prop their leg up and spit. Sometimes flickering the candle.

Yes, Mother said it was the job of the little people to tear up. To make new ways of putting things together. To keep us off balance. Otherwise we got too comfortable here and it was harder than ever to leave. Yes, it was their job to keep our eye on heaven. Even Reverend Stonesifer would agree with that.

SATURDAY

I waited in the car with Dempster and Eban while Bently went into Purdam's Gen'l Store in Haran. Even from the street I could smell the tobacco. Feedsacks. Walnut-faced dolls. Wood-carved mules. Cedar boxes. Groceries. Gasoline.

"Buick brain," Dempster said to Wylie from the front seat.

"Pig slop."

Wylie was kicking the back of the seat. "Stop it," I said to him.

The last of the yellow leaves hung to the trees behind the old brick buildings on Main Street.

"Turnip tit," Dempster said.

Inside Purdam's I could see some of Sister Whatley's quilts. The church women found them in her cabin. Maybe she'd made hundreds before she died.

"Turnip tit," Wylie repeated.

"I'll leave you with Dempster if you don't stop."

I saw the Harner brothers across the street, and scooted down in the seat. Wylie gave them the finger from the back window before I could stop him. Later, Ratsy and others from school walked by the car.

When Bently came out of the store with his sack, the boys straightened up. Bently got into the car, and we drove off in a spurt of dust. Past the storefronts on Main Street, the old gas pump, the dead tree, to old Highway 10 toward our farms on Kingdom Road in the rancid autumn air.

"They're steamin' hogs already," Bently said.

We passed the flagstone houses and rock-walled yards of Logan County. The fields full of stones and goats and turkey barns. The winding dirt roads that left the old highway and curled into the blue-hilled distance of Arkansas.

I held my arm out the window and felt the wind whip hair across my face.

Bently's Roadmaster rutting the uneven road toward the vast sky opening before heaven.

DEO GRACIAS

There biden squirrely on stick poked through the anus. Dead squirrels Rupert 'anged on crosses.

Deo gracias! Deo gracias! Adam lay ibounden in a bond for thousand winter thought he not too long.

I thought of the backwoods folks singing their dialect in church. Their underwater words. Sometimes I could sing it too, though Bently made sure we talked like the people in Fort Smith.

I had heard Mother's stories as she talked to the sorghum she stirred. Now I watched Bently turn the hog ribs soaked in Mother's sorghum and Stanley's corn whiskey. Soon I walked off toward my cousins before supper.

And all was *fo and appil that he tok as clerkes findin written in their book. Deo gracias!* Yo the bloody lamb. The sacrifice was him cut up on the cross. Not unlike another story Mother told about the Indians cutting up white people to get rid of them, to send them back into the holes in the ground where they had come from. Their tongues cut out so they couldn't talk. *Deo gracias! Deo Gracias! Ne had the appil taken ben, our Christus noten come to urth for our salvation.* Cut up like the Indians did their prey. Yey the murder of the backwoods folks on the old bloody shores of Arkansas.

Hodi Christus natus est.

Hodi Salvator apparuit.

Now snakes 'anging in the rapt. Cates and doags of Rupert's in the barn.

THE LOST TONGUE

We could split the tongues of crows and get them to talk. Eban read it in one of Bently's books. We could raise them. Take them from their mothers in the woods. Then raise them and split their tongues and they could learn to talk.

"Just like they used to," Eban said.

"Yes, we'd return their language," I agreed.

"Just like the Indian stories," Dempster said as we dug worms and put them in a Creecy Green Dry-Land Cress can in the pigeon cage out behind Stanley's work-shed while Rupert got the birds. But the birds ate themselves to death on the worms before we knew it.

Dempster found more baby crows. We didn't feed them as many worms. Eban decided when it was time to teach them to talk. Nathan holding them down opening their mouths. Dempster and Eban with Rupert gagging and squawking his voice with the crows. The blood splatting from the scissors clipping at the insides of their mouths. Nasha ran screaming through the junk into Stanley's farmhouse. Nathan tied them in a bag with only their heads sticking out. Eban pulling it tight around their necks until their tongues stuck out. Then Nathan trying to use his fishing knife clipping their tongues with the scissors again.

We thought it would take a week for them to talk. Just like those old stories Mother told about the animals talking at one time.

One time all the elements were one and we could walk up into heaven anytime we wanted. But we messed up somehow and can't go anywhere anymore. Not out behind the sun until after we died. Not even into the woods between the stars.

But the crows in Stanley's pigeon cage bled to death before they said anything. One lived for a while just sitting in the cage twerping its head to one side, its eye looking like the yellow hole of the moon.

Eban said the Indian story wasn't about animals talking after all. But about a man in the woods who put his ticker into women who left their husbands at night. That's why a little Indian blood was everywhere. That's why Bently's wife and Stanley's hushed them on the porch. Eban rubbed against me and I pushed him away.

The Indian story was about a language we had lost. And tried to get back. Maybe Rupert talked the animals' lost language when we couldn't understand him. Maybe that's what they said in church. Blabbering in new tongues. They were telling stories. New stories that were still only spoken sounds we worked to fill with meaning. Stories we tried to tell with the tongues of crows in the bottom of the cage. Stiff as grass blades the hired man cut.

COMMUNION

On Sunday we went to church when Harrison came in from the creekbottoms, his neck wrinkled as a brown sycamore leaf. We went down Kingdom Road in the truck, past Stanley's farm and Bently's toward the country church house. Harrison would close his eyes and sometimes gently rock his head during sermons. He said he didn't nap, though Bently's wife thought he did and Nasha watched him when she thought I wasn't looking.

The wind swished in the grove of fir trees outside the church house. Mother nudged me to look back to the preacher during the sermon. The cup of our Savior would be passed. But I listened to the trees and thought of Cedric.

"Te Deum," Bently always said. But it sounded like *tedium* when he said it.

"No one speaks out in church like that," Bently's wife said. "Hold your tongue."

"Hold yours."

Sometimes little white seeds passed. Cottonwood or something, and I wondered if it were Sister Whatley or others in the congregation who swooshed around in their angel-clothes just to show off to those on earth still bound with chores and hard times.

Yes Christ died for us on the cross. His body and blood left for us. Drink of it in the communion cup. Eat his bread. Drink his cup. It was the flesh of Christ we ate. The blood we drank.

I heard the hired man's boy, Rupert, behind us. He made noises sometimes that sounded like Harrison's mules, Grace and Jude, in the barnyard, though Nasha whispered to me he sounded like the crows.

Cedric almost as if he were there.

Then Reverend Stonesifer was still. The communion cup was passed through the congregation, and along the Pierces' row toward the front of the church.

"Your body and blood," Bently said.

I looked at the cup as it came toward me. Bently had the cup, then his wife, the boys, Harrison, Mother, and I—it seemed for a moment I saw the little people—at least white seeds flying again. The shore Whatley said to step back from—I heard the rip of a cover—like the tarp off the back of the truck—I looked into the cup as it came to me—*Ya kay tos*—lifted it to my mouth—I saw the blood and bits of flesh in the cup I took from Mother. They looked like pieces of the dog nearly ate by wild hogs before Harrison stopped them once. His innards all over the yard. It looked like the tongues of crows in the swill. The wine and pieces of flesh spewed from my mouth. I let the cup slip as though someone pulled it from my hand. The pewter cup spilled to the floor with a loud clunk, dark wine running suddenly across my dress like the creek. Flooding my legs, running down my shoes. I thought I saw Sister Whatley on the front row turned to stare. Mother gasped. I reached to the floor for the cup, tried to sweep the blood and flesh back into it, my hands jerked helplessly. Even Harrison spoke. He took the cup from me and passed it back to the deacon who took it to the front of the church and wiped it off and poured more wine. He returned it to Nasha beside me, Nathan, Stanley and his wife, then on to the pews behind us—

"The little peoples been loose argin," Mother said.

I had spilled the communion cup and interrupted the service. Shame burned my cheeks. Everyone looked. *For you shall not,* I remember Bently yelling at Cedric, *depart from the Lord thy God*

—shall not come between him and his blessing in our family. Everyone shifted uncomfortably in their pews. Rupert summered in his pew and had to be taken from the church.

The little church platform where Reverend Stonesifer and the small choir stood seemed to sway. The narrow church with Jesus looking from the walls gyrated. I thought we were suddenly back long ago. I smelled the altar fires. It was Jesus behind the tabernacle curtains. It was Jesus everywhere. There was no getting rid of him. I heard the animals sacrificed. The bulls and goats. Even the crows. But they were all really him.

And hadn't I, Jean Pierce, by not paying attention, come between the Lord and the congregation? I made them forget the Lord as they were parting his body, drinking his blood. It was the real blood and body they drank and ate. I saw that now. And where the varnish had worn from the uneven floor, the stain of wine went into the wood. Was there forever. So that when the Lord walked in the midst of the church He would see the stain of Jean Pierce.

"You're so clumsy, Jean," Mother scolded.

Tears washed my face. I should be brushed aside. My place taken. I felt the struggling child. Harrison squeezed my arm in embarrassment. I would spill forever with them ashamed of me, even the Lord, who forgave all sins, had to look away. I wanted someone to take me away and the child that never got born put into my place.

ABATING

Bently talked about family history one Sunday after supper as we sat around his dining room table. But I knew it already. Father and Mother Pierce had come to Arkansas by flatboat and wagon from Virginia in 1898, but they moved to Missouri after a tornado through Logan County destroyed their farm that year. Cedric sat beside me at the table. I had my foot on his under the chair. Wylie had spilled his last glass of milk, so there was nothing left to interrupt Bently.

Father and Mother had returned to Arkansas ten years after the tornado with Harrison and Bently, a handle-crank and plow. They stayed here even after the flood of 1927 covered Kingdom Road and a fifth of Arkansas.

"But the kingdom of God suffers violence," Bently read from Matthew 11:12, "and the violent take it by force." Therefore, hoisted by faith, Mother and Father Pierce retrieved what belongings they could, and shoveled mud from their farmhouse when the water abated. Then Father and Mother Pierce plowed again the coil of land along Kingdom Road and sank with their hardships under the cover of fields, birds and creaking branches the echo of their aching bones. And harvest gone, I took rise on the flock of birds from the cornfield coffin in the chilly autumn, soaring on the comfort of their toil.

After supper, Cedric and I walked through the yard, and out to the edge of the field before he left for school. Cedric held my hand and looked through the late afternoon clouds that must have been high above us. Wylie yelled for Cedric to toss him in the air, but Cedric stayed with me. Finally Dempster and Eban jumped him from behind. I fell to the ground with Cedric laughing as the boys rolled over us. He had his arms around me, and I knew we'd always be together under the trees that wrapped themselves around us, sticking us with their tongues.

Soon Nathan yelled from the field where he had trapped an animal in its burrow. I could hear Rupert clicking his mouth. Cedric and the boys went to find them, while Nasha and I sat in the yard.

When Harrison and Mother left Bently's place, I told them I'd ride back to the farm with Cedric when he left for school. It was almost dark and Cedric's mother was after him to start.

After a while, Stanley, his wife, and Nasha left Bently's place too, when Nathan and the boys came back from the field with Rupert hobbling behind them.

"Come here," Cedric said as he drove me down Kingdom Road. It was after dark and he would be late in getting back to Missouri, but he didn't seem to mind. "I want to say good-bye."

"Goody-bye, then," I said. But he pulled me over to him.

"I don't want you to leave." He stopped the car in the bushes.

"I don't want you to either."

The dark road fanned over us and I felt Cedric's arms around me and his hands in my dress. I wanted the monkey secret of Kingdom Road. I wanted Cedric's fever forever on me. He felt under my slip and underclothes for my monkey tail. But nothing was there.

"EEEEeee," I said, calling him to me. I felt his arms and legs. His back. There it was in Cedric's pants. The monkey tail. I took it in my hands and he nearly jumped over me. Closer and closer. The violent taking it by force. Sharing with me the monkey tail.

RENDERING

Nathan's corduroy trousers had a hole in them. I saw it from the back porch as I watched the men in the backyard. "He didn't need Stanley's suspenders with those pants any longer. How that boy grows." Stanley's wife fluttered in the kitchen.

The hired man's boy, Rupert, was under the table again. "Aze weard. Tuut." The eraser moved across the paper when Rupert got back in his chair.

"Gerves thwak ert goust whest aze. Ert. Ert." Rupert talked like a ghost tribe of animals.

Bently's wife told me to take him outside where Dempster and Wylie ran through the yard. Their screams mingled with the squeal of the sow. The women cooked, minded the children, yelled at the boys from the back door when they fought. I heard Wylie cry and Mother told Nasha and me to go to the creekbottoms with the boys. Rupert tagged along.

"Kiya. Duco. Duca." Rupert was tattooed inside his head. I could almost see the words written on the coils of his brain. "Baar raba."

Autumn drifted into the Arkansas valley. I smelled the smoke and wetness in the air. Along Kingdom Road, the sycamores dried and the dogwood crimped. Eban wanted to cross the hill into the other valley for blackberries.

"Don't go." I tossed a rock at Eban. "I want to stay on the farm for rendering."

"Jean was jesting with Eban." Nasha saw Wylie pick up a rock and start to throw it at Eban too.

"Throw it in the creek," I said to Wylie, and after coaxing, the rock hit the water with a splud.

Nasha tried to pick up Wylie, but he fussed and struggled until she put him down.

"I don't like rendering," Eban said as we walked along the creek while the men butchered the sow.

"What does it do?" Wylie asked him.

"Makes lard so Ma can cook."

"Whar gizz is wez tez wheezen." The hired boy said.

"Talk English, Rupert," Eban told him.

Rupert stuttered and said, "Dempster, yeur shoes wet. The mother will be fierce angry wid yeu."

Dempster laughed and Eban pushed him into the creek and Dempster chased him into the pasture.

"Er meebo." Rupert laughed so hard he wet his pants.

"They bore me," I said to Nasha.

We walked away from them toward the barn with Wylie when I saw the smoke from the rendering fire.

In the barn lot, Nasha put Wylie on Jude. Grace didn't like children but she walked with them while I watched the men. Then sun was bright in the day but I felt a sudden chill in the wind. I looked at the gray mules, Wylie's gray jacket and jeans. Nasha's eyes as they passed. The gray boards of the unpainted shed, and a pale sky through the smoke of the air.

I stood with Harrison as he took parts of the sow and melted fat from them. I watched the rendering pot long after Nasha had tired and went into the farmhouse. I saw in the crackling fire something larger than the fire. And in the rendering pot, a slow change from one form to another. I knew I would understand it someday.

While the lard that Harrison had melted cooked in the pot, we had supper at our farmhouse. The children sat in the backyard with napkins tucked under their chins. Nasha and I ate in the kitchen with Nathan and the others.

When the fat had cooled enough to pour, and the women had cleared the tables, Harrison got the buckets. It took Stanley and the hired man to tip the rendering pot while Harrison caught the running lard with the buckets. Then the women lined them along the back table, all the while telling Rupert and Dempster and Wylie to stay back. Harrison had a scar on his hand between his thumb and forefinger where the melted fat had run over his hand.

Then the work was done and Stanley always told how Mother Pierce caught her apron on fire once at rendering and Father Pierce nearly beat her to death with a horseblanket to put out the fire. Stanley had been a boy when that happened. "She walked into the farmhouse," he said, which was the one Bently lived in, "with her apron and part of her long skirt in tatters."

"Arkansas nobility." Bently always ended Stanley's tale as the afternoon moved toward night, and would move toward many nights on Kingdom Road after rendering.

The junk and wind gauges and plane parts in Stanley's yard bothered Bently. He talked to Stanley about it again. Even Harrison had an old car in the yard and an aerator that Stanley made which might have worked at one time.

Bently shook his head. "It's the result of democracy on Father Pierce's land," Bently said as they gave us cracklings from the rendering pot to eat.

And night would fall quickly in the valley as we sat in the backyard and talked, and the dew would come across the dogwood and sycamore and the fields along Kingdom Road.

"All things are undergoing change," I heard Stanley say.

"It's the cruelty of them turkey barns," Mother said.

"A farmer's got to earn a living."

"Putting things in darkness. That's the talent of our race."

Sometimes we shined a flashlight into Rupert's eyes until we thought we saw things moving there, and Rupert howled. Then the hired man and his wife would drag Rupert back kicking to their place.

Sometimes we walked down the road in the dark—Nathan, Nasha, and I, and Bently's boys after Wylie slept—and felt the universe about us.

Still they would talk into the night then gather their bowls and baskets and lard buckets and sleeping children and we'd be left in silence on Harrison's part of the land.

SOCK MOON

The evening birds flew above us, dipping sometimes to the water. They sounded like voices speaking. They sounded like noises I heard sometimes when Harrison was at his first wife's grave.

"Snakes singing with air bubbles from their throats," Mother said. "*Suggy utum* they sing. But they don't say nothing." She was quiet again as I worked on the dock, angry with Wylie who splashed us as he jumped into the water.

I looked up at the moon as the dock drifted in the cove. It was curved and thin above the three tall trees like a sock. Some blue dragonflies with balsa-wood wings revved their motors and took off toward the night.

Music buzzed across the cove and the lights bounced on the scaly water as the little waves made their way to the shore.

Mother said we could become animals. Whatever we said we could be. Anytime we could climb right out of the window and wander at night. Her stories lapped like Eban's oar in the water from the dock.

Yes, it was in the night sometimes, I could see down the road, back to my mother and me in the wagon going to her mother's, watching her ears become engorged already from the stories she would hear.

Yes, I waited also, for her stories which were breath.

It was in sleep, sometimes, when we got out of ourselves. Hadn't I heard the strange sounds at night as though others in the cabin had already gotten out of bed and were stumbling around to get dressed in the dark, but changing midair into animals. Sometimes I heard the hooves and paws across the floor as they scrambled for the window. Jumping on the sill and skittering outside. Through the wet nightgrass. Yes, and the moon was a sock dropped by the last one who passed.

THE WALK

Cedric wanted to walk down the lake road and I followed him after he left. I knew his tree in the apple orchard. I could see him far ahead. Soon I'd call his name and catch up.

In the orchard, he'd hold my head against his chest. I'd hear the tree wrap its branches around us. I'd feel his monkey tail ticking like a heart.

THE FOUNDRY

I felt the ache again for what wasn't there. Maybe it wasn't anywhere on the whole earth that rushed around the sun hot as the backwoods anger and their hard speech. They started fires in some of the cabins built along the lake road. They even tried to pull down the schoolhouse. They spat at us sometimes when we passed on the highway until the lake traffic grew heavy and they retreated farther into the woods.

Not anywhere on earth if not at the lake or farm. If we had to live without grace then space somewhere. The stars turned like Stanley's anemometers. Words broken for the first time emerged to name the world before me. The stars blue as welder's sparks in the evening sky.

The old owl, Nicodemus, Cedric gave me, a button sewn on for an eye. The button with a horse upon it for he ran until he saw the sun through the cloud's hole. And in that fiery furnace, words were just the sparks flown away that were seen and understood, forging an echo of that which came from out the furnace door. *Father, Holy Father* in the foundry of the sun, hammered iron and oars and words.

DOGWOOD

Harrison was asleep with the newspaper over his face when Bently stopped somewhere on the other side of Fort Smith. The nozzle rattled in the tank. It was empty. Bently shook his head. The gauge was broken and they guessed about the gasoline in the truck. "We could have been stranded," Harrison said, rubbing his head as they stood at the pump.

"Too bad Stanley can't fix anything practical."

Harrison talked about the price of gasoline, while Bently discussed the economy. "Creekwater runs downhill," he always said.

In the back of the truck, I had wakened when they stopped for gas. Now stiff and cramped between boxes and cousins, I was alert as they started on the highway again toward our farms. I thought about the secrets monkeys carried. I thought sometimes I saw the white flutterings of Sister Whatley in the back of the truck with us.

And I thought sometimes about Harrison and the child that had gone to the grave with its mother—fist and thigh still struggling. I felt its presence between Harrison and myself. I shivered under the tarp and tossed again.

Harrison was usually at the creek when I got to the farm after school, watering Jude and Grace, his mules; talking to her at times, his first wife, the way I talked to Cedric and Bently.

I drank at the pump from the dipper and went into the farmhouse. My mother, silent in the kitchen, stirred the kettle.

"Hello, Mother." I sat my books on the table, took off my sweater.

"'lo," she returned.

"What's for supper?"

"Ham and gravy, fried apples."

I puttered in the kitchen with my mother until supper. After we ate, washing Harrison's first wife's plates and bowl, her forks and knives, her shiny royal blue plates and bowls, dusting biscuit crumbs from the table where the first wife and Harrison sat before she died, I felt Harrison's ache.

I sat at the kitchen table after supper with my schoolwork. I watched the shadow of my hands from the kerosene lamp. The kitchen lightbulb didn't give enough light to read by, and the leaves on the wallpaper sank into the past. I thought of Cedric in the solitary farmhouse.

Was it unchristian? I thought in the church in my white voile dress. Harrison looked at me then. *She's the lily of the valley,* he said.

It was when I was older and sleep came hard that I felt the struggling fist and thigh. I kicked and snored, Harrison told me, thrashed when I slept. I woke Nasha sometimes on the cot we shared at the lake.

I thought about Cedric in the dogwood down the road. At nights in the kitchen of the farmhouse, the lack of words hungered within me.

MY CLOSET

I have to speak in school today. I stand in front of the room. I do not want to speak. I shrink nearly to the floor. I wiggle out the door of school. I swim back to my farmhouse. Down Kingdom Road. I plop across the creek. I wade in the window of my room. I hide under my bed. I see the legs of my bureau. The corner of my wooden chest. I see the bottom of my pale flowered wallpaper. Nicodemus on the floor. The shadows of my curtains blowing from the window I left open. I see my pieces of driftwood and rocks from the lake. My letters from Cedric I keep in a box under my bed. I am in my closet now. In the dark of my head. My teeth line up like icicles that hang from the roof in winter. I feel the old wooden rowboat of my tongue. I am at the entrance of my mouth. I hold my hands together. I tell my story to the dark. I speak to the two empty dresses hanging there.

RHETORING

"Harrison butchered the sow. No, first Harrison kindled the rendering fire, then he butchered the sow," I said to Bently as we talked before Sunday supper again. "He melted the fat from bacon. It hardened into lard. Thus, rendering—"

"A process by which we have a product for later use." He understood.

"Meanwhile Mother and I sowed the fallow ground of the garden. We weeded the green tomatoes, onions, celery, and dill. When they were grown, we pulled them loose from the confines of their rows—or the hired man did if we were at the lake. Then Mother and I, the other women, canned chutney, fig pickles, apple and quince, plum conserve. And we have mason jars on pantry shelves for the Arkansas winter of our hunger."

He smiled.

"On cold nights, Mother fries bread with the lard Harrison rendered, and she greases the supper kettle for the opossum stew," I said. "She cooks potatoes, cabbage, parsnips, black-eyed peas, salt pork, and opens a jar of chutney from the shelf."

"That's rendering!" Bently said.

"A process of occupying," I said and Bently folded his arms. "Sometimes I think of the muxing," I told Bently. "Lard from the rendering pot, and potatoes from Mother's garden rows, intersect in the supper kettle. Likewise, images from outward sources, ideas from within, come together." I struggled to understand. "I order the images and ideas. Arrange them. Adapt their different parts to a whole. The creative spark—the feeling I have at the fire under the rendering pot—the stuff of *thinking it out,* Bently— rhetoring—or whatever its name, is under it—heating it up—has been under it since idea and image first came. Maybe it was the fire that first brought them forth."

He was astounded, he said, rubbing his hands.

"And you see, Bently, rendering only gives Harrison lard, not the supper," I said. "And rhetoring, though it seems complete within itself and is—prepares the way for other rhetorings."

"From that process, other processes come."

"Exactly," I agreed. I had been afraid that Bently's wife would call us into the dining room before I finished, but I had reached the point I wanted to make.

"And why all the rhetoring? Why all the bother?" he asked.

"So that I won't hunger. I can't stand it, Ced—Bently," I corrected, "when thoughts aren't with me. I feel shut away in the farmhouse. I feel sometimes I'll be pulled off the edge of the earth. But rhetoring generates. It keeps me here."

Bently folded his arms and listened to me.

"I will always be able to grease the supper kettle," I said. "My pencil is like that stick at the church house which they used to tap those who fell asleep during the sermons."

Bently laughed. "So that we recognize our privileged hour in the church house, Father Pierce said."

"For me, writing and thinking are similar to going to church," I told him. "It's the hungering of the self for the other—for God. In the instance of the unbeliever, it's the struggle to be one's own god—by the creative act."

"And what do you think about speaking?" Bently asked.

"Not much," I said. "You know, Bent—you know how I ran. I felt my face lift like a black snake from under the step to the shed."

"You'll get over it—"

"No," I said. "It was—placing a world into the structure of my words. It was something like the touch between two terrible hands."

THE UNWILLING LORD AND THE RISING CREEK

Daniel stood at the back door, his heavy apron stained. He smelled of coal smoke.

He came to Haran's backwoods school with Bently.

Stanley taught him to weld.

He turned his cap backward, pulled the shield over his face, lifted wheel to Stanley's drum.

Sparked lightning from the east, spanned gorges, hills.

His eyes the flames of holy fires.

He welded wheel to oil drum.

THE BACKWOODS SCHOOL

Bently visited his students in the rugged hollows of Arkansas where the dialect could hardly be understood. One afternoon I went with him down a narrow, two-rut path. "It's been a while since a car passed on this road," I said. "Maybe you should walk."

"We'll make it," Bently assured.

His new Roadmaster jumped like a pogo stick, but Bently pursued his course. Then at one point the tire-ruts sank and Bently's tan Buick with "Fort Smith" on the front bumper ran aground on the hump between the ruts.

Bently's wife had asked him why he didn't have "Haran" instead of "Fort Smith" since that's where he lived.

"At least the road's not muddy," I said.

Bently tried to back up, but the Buick snorted and hopped as he put it in reverse—forward—reverse.

"They'll know we're coming," I said.

Bently got out of the car and pushed while I tried to drive it backward. He showed me how to rock the car, and with Bently's shove with each backward heave, I backed it off the hump between the ruts.

I waited in the car on the road while Bently walked down the ruts to make his call. I knew he would be a while and I was reading a schoolbook when he returned.

"They stay isolated from America," he explained, getting back in the car. "Their superstitions—their horseshoes over their doors to ward off evil spirits." Bently snorted. But even Harrison carried a buckeye against rheumatism.

"Maybe not all changes are able to be made," I supposed. "They ran you off the place?"

"Close to it." Bently rubbed his hands and started the car.

I think he came nearer to getting shot.

Bently was a crusader in the backhills of Arkansas. "I want to give people meaning," he said, but the people around Haran and the backwoods school at the lake didn't seem to want it.

MY COVE

It had rained all spring. The Osage River, usually nothing more than a creek, had rushed under Plimsoll Bridge when we came to the lake. And the ramp to our dock was jammed against the shore by the barrels that were pushed up in the high water. The *Commodore,* half-submerged in the boat-shed, had been eaten through with termites.

"I should have looked at her last winter," Stanley said, "when I was here on a hunting trip."

"She wouldn't have floated this year anyway," I told Nathan. "Her wood was rotten." Nathan pulled the old wooden rowboat on the shore with the debris the high water brought to the cove.

The rain continued until the backwoodsmen stayed along the porch-rail in the small lake town to talk. The men at Salmer's Landing thought it was the wettest summer they could remember, wetter than the dry summers had been dry. They shook their fists above them and still there was rain.

After supper I went down to the shore in the rain, thumping my twig on the boards of the dock with the rain that pattered on the barrels underneath. With my twig I dredged the puddled edge of the cove. Weeds and wetclumped leaves came up, shiny as the silk of old umbrellas.

Nathan came down to the cove and tied the rotted hull of the *Commodore* on the shore. The locks at the dam had been opened to ease the water in the lake, and the debris along the shore would float back into the lake. Then when Cotter, the town below the dam, and the farms began to flood, the locks would be closed, and back would come the driftwood and debris to the shores of the lake.

I sat on the hill in the late afternoon and watched the clouds across the main channel of water. I felt hunger again. The ache for words. I looked for Bently to talk to but he had gone somewhere in the boat, and Cedric hadn't come to the lake yet.

I moved Nicodemus and got my journal from the wooden chest and looked from the window of the cabin, but the leaves were in the way. I went back to the hill and looked again at the sky.

As I watched the clouds low on the horizon, they looked like hills, and the sky beneath them looked like the lake.

I looked at the sky. Holy Lord. I lay back on the hill with my hands to my head and sat up again. The clouds and the sky made an image of the hills and the lake! I saw an image of the lake in the sky, the lake with its coves. And there in the sky was one particular cove that stood out in the clouds. I put my hands to my eyes and took them away again.

The lake in the sky was still there.

SPATE

Cedric was at the cabin when I came up the hill one afternoon. Eban had just left in Bently's boat. I wanted to run to Cedric but instead I waved and went into the cabin. When I saw him walking down the hill with Harrison and Nathan, I took some trash down for the fire.

The logs from the high water smoldered on the shore. Harrison had towed away some of the larger logs. The smaller ones and the debris that didn't float away when the water went down were burned as soon as they dried. The *Commodore* had gone in one of the fires.

"'lo," I said to Cedric. His hair was thinner but otherwise he was the same. I had written long letters to him and he had returned to Haran in the winter, but it had been a while since I'd seen him.

Harrison talked about the high water and pointed to the waterline on the boat-shed when he went for the gas can. Nathan and I had used all the gasoline for a boat ride, which I knew Harrison had just discovered.

"I'll go to the landing for you," I said. Harrison wanted to keep the logs burning. He would sprinkle them with gasoline now and then.

"All right," he said, "since it was you that used it."

"Come with us, Cedric," I said. But Nathan didn't want to go. He would rather fish. So Cedric and I got into Harrison's boat and pushed away from the dock.

I wanted to talk to Cedric but the boat was too loud. I pointed to a clearing in the woods where another cabin was being built, but Cedric didn't understand.

I turned into Salmer's Landing for gas and filled Harrison's gallon tank. "There're still some coves that haven't been cleared," I said.

We returned to our dock with the gas and Cedric pushed away again. I started out across the lake.

Cedric said something about Eban but I couldn't hear him in the roar of the motor and I shrugged my shoulders at him.

"I thought I'd seen Eban," Cedric said as we came into a vacant cove from the choppy lake, "but I guess it wasn't him."

"There are so many boats now on Bull Shoals," I brought the boat into the rough shore. "Jump out, Cedric, and catch that rope."

He got out of the boat and tied the rope to a stump by a large rock. We climbed the ledge together.

"I missed you, Cedric," I said.

"I missed you too, Jean." Cedric hugged me.

"The grass we're sitting in is turkeyfoot," I said then, leaning back in his arm. "See it strut in the wind. It makes me think of the turkey farms all over Arkansas—just now hatching so we can be thankful."

He laughed and kissed me.

"I wish I had my pencil, don't let me forget."

"I won't."

"Haven't you missed the lake?"

Cedric looked out across the water.

I said, "The lake is bigger to me, even than it really is. It spilled over to the sky where I found my cove." I had written to him about it. "You know how I was always looking?"

He nodded.

"I see my cove on certain evenings when the clouds hover on the horizon and the sun goes down behind them. I see an image of the lake and hills in the sky."

Cedric kept looking across the lake and didn't say anything for a while. I leaned my head on Cedric's shoulder while he thought. Presently he talked about the university where he went to graduate school and taught. He wasn't much older than his students. I was in Haran's high school, I regretted, as he talked about some of the books he taught.

"I want words too," I said. "Words that heat up everyone around them like the rendering fire, like the potbellied store in Purdam's Gen'l Store in Haran, and plain as the handprinted sign. I want words like the dirt roads in town I can feel under my feet. Words should move things around like the little people."

Cedric looked at me and said nothing.

"Words to me are like the logs and mortar of our cabin. I always wanted a stone fireplace, Cedric, but Harrison never built one. We aren't here so much in the winter anyway." I said, "Cedric, you can build a stone chimney for our cabin and shoot an elk for over the mantel."

"Jean, I never know what you're going to say," Cedric said, taking his arm from around me.

"Let's talk about words again," I said in the lapping waves that quickened after boats passed on the lake. "I think they're little sparks of light. Little energy fields that make the lake and its coves in our head. My mother's mother said that once. Or something like it. I want to be a visionary, Cedric, only into that which is old."

Cedric was silent.

"I'm going to rise in his arms someday and you're going to be at the gate still arguing with God that he can't be known empirically." I gathered my thoughts again. "I read Obadiah, James, and the woodchips fly."

Cedric smiled. "Yes, Reverend Stonesifer's preaching was like an ax."

"It gets back to copying, doesn't it?" I asked. "But I don't want to wander in my own darkness. I want his light for my feet."

"It's a matter of preference," Cedric said.

"It's a matter of your trying to beat the creator with his own invention, Cedric," I answered.

LAND HO!

The pages of my journal were high waters of my cove printed with widening circles of rain that came and went on the shore that summer, raising my own waters to a lake's spill over the edge of the earth. Er meebo. Gert. Whez.

Columbus of the clouds in journals of rope untied from shore. The lake moved across the horizon, took flight. As earth traveled the sky, I record the journey, making space of rain puddles.

Waters rise on the umbrella frame of feet. The waters part, back into that which was old before the foundation of the earth. In church and along the dust road. Beside it there is no other place. The congregation sings, not recording their journey. They must understand what I don't. A winding mark through the clouds was the lake road through the hills.

Land ho!

My cove in the sky.

ELECTRIC STORM

In the fall Stanley wired the church house in Haran. Reverend Stonesifer could have church now on Sunday and Wednesday nights without the kerosene light. But rain got into the walls and the church house danced with blue lights.

"The Holy Ghost," Bently's wife yelled.

"Glory to God." Mother's mouth hung open like Sister Whatley's had.

"The end of the world," I heard Eban cry.

"Stanley reversed the lightning rod!" Bently hit his knee and hawed.

The walls of the church house hopped with static electricity. The blue lights twittered like the anemometers on Stanley's farm. The whole place was lit. Sparks jumped from lightbulbs, eerie and blue as those across the broken water of the lake that ripped with scales and turned reptile in the night.

I heard the monkey screams from the walls.

Nasha hid her eyes.

It was like the time Harrison's radiator overheated and he

didn't have a funnel and Stanley said water especially creek-water followed a stick and he stuck the stick in the hole of Harrison's radiator and the creek-water ran all over the generator and little beads of water hopped and fizzed.

The blue triangles of electricity jumped like Stanley's haybale lifter in Harrison's barn.

"Worse than Stanley's manure conveyor," Harrison said.

The blue lights hissed. We could go anytime. The place was ripe for harvest. Nasha held onto me quivering. Dempster and Wylie cried. I heard the people speak in tongues. I heard them scream it was the translation.

Reverend Stonesifer seized the moment. He walked on the rug between the aisles and fire seemed to rise in his footsteps. "Sinner repent," he said.

The men hunched like buzzards in their pews. The ones I saw in Haran with cigarettes in their mouths. Skinny, hunched-over men who beat their farm animals or didn't water them. Men you couldn't look at or they'd say, "Need a squeeze, sister?" While their poor wives and scrawny brats sat home with their fingers in their noses.

It seemed the whole church was blazing with the brushfires Harrison set in the ditches of his fields.

Reverend Stonesifer was going at a pitch. They had some poor backwoodswoman on the floor. She had tried to leave her husband who hit her and the children, who drank up all the money, who raped the animals. Yes she was a sinner-woman. The deacons and elders prayed that she bear her burdens. That she come under the yoke. That she submit to her husband like the gospel said.

Hussy woman, Reverend Stonesifer said. Intelligence was wickedness. The will itself was sin. A hot viper ready to strike. Hallelujah. The elders and deacons held her to the rug. The flames were probably scorching her back. We weren't to think. But to obey. That was the ultimate test. To do what we wanted was transgression. There was a stalk of evil in us. It had to be uprooted. We would stop at nothing. No measure was too harsh. *Come out of her,* they yammered. Keep her on the narrow path. Lord all other ways are contrary to your law. All others ways that seemed right were only death. DEATH. Reverend Stonesifer's voice screeched again. And suddenly the church house went dark. Not dark really. Afterlights burned. Ghosts or echoes of the lights that had hopped all over the church. Just like monkeys in their cage.

The whole place was wild with noise. I could see it like a herd of butterflies in the rows of goldenrod on Harrison's farm. It flew all over just for pollen. Oh look at the walls of the church. The afterlight in the border of goldenrod. The flagmen from the spirit world!

I heard Nasha speaking in tongues beside me. I felt Nathan and Eban jump up and down. Lord knows where Bently's wife was. I felt the sweaty wetness of Wylie all over me and Mother sat quiet at my side.

"We're talking like the animals," she said.

Reverend Stonesifer didn't stop. His voice was like Harrison's backfiring truck. A mutant hybrid race of birds was loose in the church. And monkeys shrieking their secret. We had once had intelligence but used it for EVIL. Yes we did. So that's why we thacked around in our empty heads now. We could obey and not think. That's what we were here for. But there was some of it left. We had to be careful and pull it out. The old giant race of people were now mutants. Monkeys in God's sight. Banished to Africa. We actually brought them back. But all things work for good. Yes there are no mistakes in God's kingdom. Those old sinners were right here in Arkansas. Like the monkeys in Little Rock's zoo. Right here for us to see and to remember what could happen to us.

And yez, Mother said, *we knew it was coming.* They were led by a woman, the monkeys were, and we were not going to let that happen again. It was HER that got us into trouble going wayward and contrary-wise to the given order, the god-ordained holy-spirit spoke god-worshipping order. Wagonloads of trouble. That's what a woman was.

Yez the monkeys were refugees of the old war. They had been a giant race of men. Weren't they in the Bible yez they were. Their remnants were mostly in Africa now the mother of sin. They would try to jungle-ate the world again. Darkness. Evil Darkness. Evil Africa. Hollow Seat of Sin.

Reverend Stonesifer seemed frantic now, trying hard to get the message through—men had gone haywire and short-circuited and were kept forever hopping like static electricity with sin. That was the monkey secret.

But Christ was stuck like a sow on the cross so we would be free of that old cavorting. His blood and flesh still floated in our communion cup so we would know the truth. All that wickedness in the backhills right up to—YES—butted against the shore of heaven we almost touched.

THE CABIN

"Go slower, Jean," Nasha said. "You scare me."

"I scare myself sometimes," I answered.

We were on our way back to our cabin after Nasha flowered her skirt at the schoolhouse. "Flared skirt," the boys laughed at the red spot behind Nasha. I wanted to go back to the cabin anyway, hoping I would have a letter from Cedric.

"What do you want to be?" I asked Nasha as we drove down the road. "I want to be a streamer from the Maypole at the backwoods school and fly across the sky," I said before I gave Nasha a chance to answer. "But it's too frightening, not having a Maypole."

"I want to be a missionary," Nasha said, and I turned onto our lake road in laughter.

Stanley's wife was washing the windows of the cabin when we came up the road. She had wispy hair like the feather duster on the peg at Purdam's Gen'l Store in Haran. She fussed whenever a car came up the road and stirred the dust. I waved at her.

Nasha got out of the car and ran to her mother, clutching the back of her skirt. Stanley's wife was like a wren, I thought, closing the empty mailbox. "By the Lord," she said on the ladder when I got out of the car, "somehow we'll get along." I saw Wylie with a bandage on his head. "It was the car Stanley built," she shook her head, and went into the cabin with Nasha.

Nasha, in a clean skirt, didn't want to return to school. We sat on the porch by Wylie as he told us about his accident that morning. Stanley had built a car for him which was nothing more than a box on wheels. It would roll slowly down Kingdom Road. Stanley put it in the back of his station wagon and they drove into a steep hill in Haran, oiled its wheels, but it still wasn't fast enough for competition. They brought it back to the farm and Stanley put an anemometer on the back of it. Nathan got an old license plate from the junkyard that Stanley frequented for parts to his inventions. Then Stanley brought it to the lake where Dempster pushed it down the hill with Wylie in it. The car came to a stop against a tree, and the country doctor had taken fifteen stitches in Wylie's head after we had left for school.

Stanley's wife hung Nasha's skirt on the line. Nasha blew her nose.

I sat with her and Wylie by the creel for a while. I watched Stanley's wife wash the windows in short movements. Her broom was at the back door, the straws had curled up and worn to a half-moon.

I washed the rutabaga in the basin that my mother would prepare for supper. There was always cooking and washing and cleaning for the twelve or thirteen Pierces that were usually at the cabin. Bently's wife was often angry with me because I wouldn't help.

I would do better, I thought, and told Nasha that I would watch Wylie with her.

IT WON'T BE FOR EVERYONE

Stanley thought he had his plane. The lights of Harrison's truck shined in the yard as Nathan and Stanley worked into the night.

The window shut to the women in the farmhouse.

We'd gone by truck. Bently and his wife had been on a train. Mother and I had gone to Little Rock on the bus when I was small to visit her aunt who died.

Before that we'd gone on the bus to see her mother in the country. Taking a wagon after the bus let us off. The little spirits popping their white seeds in my mouth and ears. I felt them rush every opening.

But now we would make awkward leaps at the sky. We'd been in enough bus stations. Now there was a landing strip close to Haran.

"Of course the plane won't be for everyone," I told Cedric, who was at Stanley's farm that night. Nathan's girlfriend had talked with us also, but she got bored and went in the farmhouse with the women.

Cedric stood with me by the tree in Stanley's yard as the men worked. I was wrapped in a blanket, held my hands to my ears when Stanley started the motor of his plane. But soon it quit and I could see the men working on the engine again in the dark. Sometimes I thought I could even see Mother's little people in the yard, running back and forth between the lights. Even Rupert yelped to them.

Cedric was back from the university in Missouri for Thanksgiving and I wanted to be with him before he left again. "What is up there, Cedric?" I asked as we looked into the dark sky by the tree. "Mother and Father Pierce and Harrison's first wife and child traveling through the night?" Cedric didn't say anything. "Maybe they're working on Plimsoll Bridge up there and can smell the chimneysmoke along the road." I saw that Cedric didn't want to talk.

"Sometimes I dream about Sister Whatley. I can almost see her in heaven—swatting angels in the night. Someday I'll see her again—out beyond the sun."

"I don't believe in God."

"I know. I've heard Bently yell," I said. "But you have a place you go."

"The apple orchard," he said. "I only went there because there were too many people at our cabins. Whenever I felt my fever coming back, I'd go there."

"I like everyone in the family around me, Cedric. You should try to live at my farmhouse without them," I answered. "But I want a place. I want to believe."

"Don't look too hard, Jean—you'll end up living with a brain the size of Arkansas," he said. We were quiet while Stanley had his engine going again. I had my head on Cedric's shoulder and he held me in the dark. "I think about God," I said to him when it was quiet again, "with Bently standing before him."

Cedric took his hand from my back.

"And God is widening the road in heaven and Bently is telling God how it ought to be done and God is listening, rubbing his chin as he takes counsel from Bently."

Cedric laughed.

In the truck lights though the dark I saw Stanley hit the airplane with his rag and Harrison told him to quit for the night, and called me home with him.

"It's being willing to step into the sky and say, where are you, God?" I said.

"And being prepared to wait." Cedric took his other hand from my shoulder.

"It's being willing to let your spirits loose in the dark with the crows, and know a sky will be there."

THEY'VE ALREADY DONE IT

Dempster and Wylie and I were on the dock as I sat under my tree on the hill with my journal. I listened to them jump in the water and yell at one another. Wylie hated the tree by my window where he'd been tied on a long rope when he was little so he wouldn't wander off. But in those dirt clods under my swing, I traveled around the sun with my twig. For him the tree had been a whipping post; for me, sitting under my swing, making marks in the dirt, had been a beginning.

I saw Stanley come from the boat-shed followed by Bently with a load of Stanley's junk. Stanley would collect his bedsprings and fulcrums and crampons on the hill and in the boat-shed until Bently would rage, and Stanley would have to haul off his usables again.

I junked some of my ideas too as I sat on the hill with my journal. Yet the words came back again. I wrote, put the notebook aside in frustration, watched Stanley and my cousins; but soon I had the pencil in my hand again, like Stanley, collecting something where nothing had been.

LAUGHTER OF RABBITS

"It's been done before," Bently's wife said to Stanley as they worked on his airplane in the yard.

But Stanley persisted with the vehicle for his inward vision.

It was, after all, the inventor that plowed with twigs, endured aloneness to mark the fields and leaf fires, and with a roar of his engine, Stanley jumped across the furrows.

"I thought you'd have seen the boys on Kingdom Road," Bently's wife said another Saturday afternoon when we were together. "And it's nearly supper."

"No, we didn't see them," Bently said on the porch. We'd just gotten back from a walk.

"Do you know where your brothers are?" Bently asked Eban as he passed.

"No."

I snapped green beans in the basin for supper as I sat on the porch with Mother, Bently, and his wife. The apples were already in the creel, the potatoes and corn roasting in a smoldering pile of old leaves.

"Stanley and his family went to Haran," Mother said. "Don't do too many of them beans."

"Did they fly or drive?" Bently's wife asked.

Red cloth on the table, the round plates of our faces look at the other across the fields of kale and chard. We know the rabbits are in the beans. We do not speak of it. Silence is about us like the old sweater Mother wears, buttons not in the proper hole. But they don't always have to go together: precise thought to word, and word to gesture over the plate of red beans and fur. Even now, we connect like rabbit's hands.

THE WEDDING

Early on a summer Saturday I rode down Kingdom Road in the truck between Harrison and Mother to the church in Haran. Nasha and I and Bently's boys would stand with Nathan as he married. His wife-to-be had a wedding party that nearly filled the church by itself. Our family and hers and all their friends. A low branch tugged at the truck like Mother's hands at my cambric dress she'd made. I held a flat straw hat that trailed ribbons.

Cars were parked along the road by the box elders. Harrison pulled into a space between two cars by a Holub's Tobacco sign that had been nailed to one of the box elders. Mother clicked her tongue at the sign.

Bently and his wife stood on the steps of the church. I walked past them into the vestibule and stood with Stanley and his wife as the wedding guests arrived. I held the lily of the valley and watched people shuffle into the church. Soon Harrison and Mother, Bently, and his wife came in.

A girl lit the candles while the last of the guests were seated in the crowded church. Nathan's bride came from the corner room with her parents and I felt a fervency that made me long for Cedric.

When the piano began, I felt like I had when I went to the Fort Smith civic orchestra with Bently and the others, and we sat before the violas that shined like Stanley's chestnut mare in the field. I felt the turning wind gauges on Stanley's farm as the mare ran.

Stanley and his wife were seated on the front row, then Nathan's mother-in-law.

When I got to the altar I turned and watched the others coming down the aisle. For some reason, my heart pounded in my chest. Soon Nathan's wife-to-be came down the aisle with her father. Then I turned back to the altar with the others and faced Reverend Stonesifer. The candles sparkled in the sun that came in the windows and I smelled the lily of the valley.

"Who gives this woman in marriage?" Stonesifer asked.

"Her mother and I," the father answered.

I saw the ribbons tremble on the flat straw hat the girl beside me wore. I knew mine were trembling also as Reverend Stonesifer prayed and began the wedding vows. The ribbons were red as the communion wine I remembered. We drank the awful blood because Christ wanted to marry us. Yes, he was the bridegroom.

Once in a while a child cried out or someone coughed. The candles seemed to brighten and a presence filled the church.

"Do you, Nathan, take this woman—"

A child cried out again and was taken from the church. I could hear it yelling from the row of box elders. But Nathan and his wife-to-be repeated their wedding vows as though nothing sounded in the church. Her voice was soft as pencil lead on paper. They looked at one another as if ready for the years ahead.

I felt the presence again as I stood in the church and listened to the voices.

He's the lily of the valley
the haze on early fields—

I thought I would cry at the altar beside the others and I saw the girl next to me turn once. I felt another presence then too, the child who had not been born always struggling for my place. I saw the sun in a haze through the window and the candles shimmied. I felt terror again. I felt I would be taken. A shiver went up my spine as though I would be lifted from my body. I fought to hold my place. I heard Reverend Stonesifer pray for me and the candles stopped their shaking. Yes when Christ came near us he was hot as the rendering pot. I saw his arms reach toward me. Yes he could burn us with his fire and we were not consumed. Yes he could burn us with his fire and we were his. We entered his kingdom. He showed us story upon story. The floors of heaven went on forever. Our feet dancing across them. Trotting. Outside, there were people trying to hop into heaven like rabbits that tried to jump the hired man's fence into the garden. But none could get in unless they had the last name of Christ. Yes we were called the very name of God. We were blessed. I saw how swiftly events moved to their end. Hallelujah Lord God. And Lord Christ who lived with God. Yes, they shared their land with the Holy Ghost. One day we would rise in the skies and go to our bridegroom's house. We could endure torture for him. Heaven would roll back like a scroll. Over whatever the rough lake. The wind dried up and the dry land appeared.

I stood beside the girl whose ribbons trembled more than ever. Though everyone looked at me, Reverend Stonesifer continued the ceremony.

"You have made your vows in the presence of Almighty God and of these witnesses." Reverend Stonesifer was finishing the ceremony.

I felt the chestnut mare again, and the wind gauges, as he prayed. Then Nathan and his wife turned before the wedding guests and walked up the aisle together. I dried my tears and followed.

"I didn't know if you were going to make it," Bently said to me in front of the church where we stood and spoke with people who walked past us into the yard. Some of them stopped to look at me.

"Sure I was," I answered as Mother and Harrison, the other Pierces, went by to wait in the yard for the early wedding supper. The tables in the yard were under a canopy of fir trees. The churchwomen hurried to carry the meal to the tables as Nathan and his wife laughed with their guests.

God would place us in heaven where he wanted us. We would please God forever, I thought as I watched them work. Yes that was our job. That was the secret of the monkey cage. If I opened the locked door, I would be less than I would with God. I would think, not like Cedric who had thought his way out of heaven, but I would think of heaven, write about it until it was where I wanted to be. I would show Cedric the way. I had felt him during the wedding. I think it had been my ceremony after all.

"Jean, dear," Bently's wife rushed up. "I thought you were going to faint. Whatever on earth was shaking you?" she asked.

I stood with my hands still holding the lily of the valley and didn't know what to say. Soon she rushed on to someone else.

There was a shy wife in the church yard after the wedding. I watched her through the crowd. Her small children clung to her, as insecure as their mother. The children bothered her. She tried to get them to let go of her but they held to her skirt, pushed the other, stepped on her feet, whined, wiped their noses.

"Sister Chedester from Pea Ridge," I asked Bently about her because I hadn't seen her before.

"One of my wife's sisters married a clodhopper," Bently said afterward when he and Dempster and I were standing by ourselves. "It was her daughter."

"What do you mean, clodhopper?" I asked. "Aren't you one of the family?"

"You're the same stuff also," my uncle returned.

Dempster looked resentful as he stood with Bently. He had been in trouble with some boys from Haran and it angered Bently. He had also wrecked Bently's boat. I thought it must be Dempster's punishment to stay with Bently.

"Can I go yet?"

"Not yet," Bently said.

Sister Chedester was afraid to bother her husband. She saw him talking to a group of men by the road. She must have thought he would be angered by her approach. He seemed to be content to ignore her as he talked with the men. She moved toward him, then decided not to go. She was awkward and miserable in the crowd with her puling children.

Bently's wife, arms straight to her sides, came to him about some matter, probably Wylie and a friend running through the people, big as they were now, bumping into wedding guests, or fighting at the edge of the church yard.

"Go on—" Bently threatened Dempster, and he ran off through the crowd.

"You're always taking matters into your own hands," I heard Bently say to his wife as he followed her through the crowd in the other direction.

I saw Nathan and his wife, the others. I stood a while in the church yard with people still looking at me.

Mother was at the cemetery fence and I knew Harrison was in the graveyard.

Across from the church, I saw the row of box elders. I had not understood them in the years I'd gone to Haran's church. Their leaves were different from the firs and maples. Now their meaning enlarged for me. I stood in the church yard like those trees. Now I felt marked with Holub's sign.

I knew almost everyone. I talked with the Haran folks who stared, and listened to the language of the wedding guests as the women sat the early supper in the yard.

Give me oil in my lamp
keep my burning—

A child danced in the church yard, twirling around and around. Her dark socks bagged on her thin legs. Her checkered dress was too short, the sash undone. She wore the heavy shoes of the hill folks. I gave her my lily of the valley when she quit twirling and she ran somewhere into the crowd.

Art should be kinetic, bound to family, others. It should never be apart. Art was a similitude. The Christ-mind in the church yard. The words I heard in church, the noonday supper in the yard, that was rhetoric. Art brought me down to the dirt road, to the box elder trees. I stood in the church yard with the others. Wasn't that the way the Lord had gone? Wasn't I to follow? My art in its beginnings was like those children clinging to their mother.

I went to meet Sister Chedester as the wedding guests took their places at the tables.

THE UNIVERSITY

I started to the University of Arkansas in the fall. It was built across a steep hill like our cabin at the lake. I walked up Buchanan Street to class and returned to the rooming house with an orange pumpkin, which was later stolen, at the door. After supper I talked a while, then studied.

I had words within me—like a struggling fist and thigh—like trees on the hill that groped with their own uncovering.

We talked again on the front porch of the rooming house one night. Cars parked on the steep hill. The noises of students passed now and then.

Inside I had a room with a girl named Jencie. Some of her friends shared their voices with the night, alive with enough of its own sounds.

"Coyote woman in a hairnet." One of the boys made sport of me.

"I am not coyote woman."

Rags piled up along the road, hills swirled. I saw faces in the fields like primitive visions of people in trees.

She's got more leaves than me, yellow spidery ones, fat reds.

"You won't even dance, Jean Pierce," the boy said.

"She doesn't know how," his friend answered.

I burned with embarrassment. I wanted to dance with him, talk to him, anything but go back into the room and be alone. I could think I was with Cedric, like Harrison talking to his first wife in the morning haze in the creekbottoms. But it wasn't Cedric I was with.

Yet I had faith we would be together. Reverend Stonesifer

hadn't preached to me for nothing all those years. *Though it was a sin, Harrison Pierce, to let her go to the university,* Reverend Stonesifer said, I was going to school to learn like Cedric had. I was going to be monkey-brained.

Like small animal skeletons I found after snow, faith is rural and mule-stubborn. Image, idea, metaphor, concept, pushed down, pressed together until it is transfigured like the Christ.

WINTER CLOTHES

Cedric had not come back to the farms the past summer after I finished high school in Haran and I longed for him. I had walked down the road kicking dust and sat by the creek while Nathan fished. It wasn't until I returned to the farm from Fayetteville for my winter clothes that I saw Cedric again.

Bently's wife got out of the car in the drive of our farm. I saw from the upstairs window in Mother's bedroom that Cedric was in the car and I went downstairs.

"Ah getting them ready for winter," Bently's wife was saying to Mother, "and you just have one child." She had brought a dress that Stanley's wife had made for me, and showed Mother the flannel shirts that Stanley's wife had made for her boys. "I've been out all day."

She held her arms straight to her sides as she talked, like she did when she was upset with the boys. She always seemed out of step, but she was convinced it was the way everyone should be.

"If Bently gets killed—" She said about him flying with Stanley, who still tried to get his plane off the ground.

"We'll bury him in the Buick," Mother said under her breath.

"We're in a hurry," she told me, and I went on past her to the front door with my coat.

Cedric got out of the car and I stood before him in the farm-yard in the chilly valley.

"Thank you for all your letters, Cedric. I couldn't have gotten along without them."

"I can't stay long, Jean," Cedric answered. "Mother and Eban are anxious to get back to the house."

"I could go with you—"

"No," he said determinedly. "Jean," he paused, "I'm going to be married."

The words startled me and I stiffened before him.

"I'm too old for you and we're cousins—"

"We don't have to have children, Cedric. Age doesn't matter."

"Yes it does, Jean."

Eban sat in the car watching us. I knew Bently's wife would soon return as tears filled my eyes.

Sorrow gushed like cold water from the pump in the backyard. I washed my face when Cedric was gone, but cried again.

When Harrison came back from the creekbottoms, I went to Haran with him. Harrison gave me his handkerchief and I hid my face in it.

"Harrison, I loved him, though he's my cousin."

He didn't say anything, but I knew he listened.

We drove past houses. The trees, leaf-blown, bent and gnarled with knotted limbs down the hill into Haran. Jarred by a ruthole, I thought of Bently's farmhouse torn last winter because he was making another room to separate Dempster and Wylie.

The brick stores on Main Street stood together and commerce was bullish.

"'lo there, Jean," Foquot said.

Harrison bought what he'd come for in Purdam's, and we started back up the hill.

The inventor sees in metaphors, understands the icy fields in Fayetteville, ditch-grass stiff as words when they are first formed in the cold of thought.

I thought in words that cooked sometimes to nothing in the supper kettle, had to go to mason jars on pantry shelves again, endure hardship, unlike the variety of black-eyed peas that went to mush in the salt pork and parsnips, as I worked on the parts of my vehicle, searched for form.

I wrote the scrub oaks and trees at the lake. The birds and scurrying animals. I heard them under the cabin at night. The sound of the water lapping, the fishing boats and trawlers out on the lake. The rocks talking. Listen Cedric to the stories they tell.

MOTHER TURNED HERSELF INTO A ROCK AND SLEPT

Traffic moved faster on the steep hills and sharp curves of the Arkansas mountains. I had Harrison's truck going faster than it ever had gone. The tarp flopped behind us.

"Slow down, Jean," Harrison said.

Mother was sick and I was returning to the farm from Fayetteville. I was in the middle of classes when he came for me.

We passed Sturdevant's, the junk man, who Stanley had talked with in the year that Nathan had gone to the university.

I kept south on the interstate when we neared Fort Smith and the cars passed Harrison's old truck. We were the slow vehicle then. We passed a hitchhiker that Harrison would have picked up in former years.

A road sign for Porum Landing and Muldrow pointed across the Arkansas River where the prairie drifted into the flat land of Oklahoma. We were silent as Harrison watched the traffic.

We drove through Fort Smith, up the steep hill on Garrison

from the river. We followed an old truck on the highway toward Haran for several miles until I could pass.

"Stanley brought the wood," Harrison said, his first words since Fort Smith. I saw it stacked on the porch as we passed the farmhouse below us, then turned into our drive at the curve. My winter clothes that Mother had stored in tobacco were on the line in the backyard. They must have been there for several days.

How did she do it without words? I thought as I saw Mother in her bed. She made for us from the land with the yellow leaves falling about her. In her fever, her gray head, like the gray road, left the farm, though she'd never been anywhere like the road, nor connected with others. She talked, slept, mumbled in her sleep as I sat with her. I knew it was probably the little people she talked to, or her mother.

I cooked supper for Harrison under the kitchen leaves on the yellowed walls. He ate at the table by himself, then passed the room where Mother was. The road cut into the hills without asking. I thought I saw Dempster pass on the road from Mother's window, but it seems I'd heard Harrison say that Dempster had wrecked Bently's new Buick Roadmaster, and he couldn't go anywhere.

I would have at least words, I thought as I sat by my mother's bed where thin curtains hung from the long narrow windows. Her room was small. There was a bureau and the rumpled bed.

I felt the struggling fist and thigh. I wanted to be back at school with my journal. I wanted to be worthy of my stain on the church house floor. I knew at times I should quit the university and stay with Mother and Harrison. They only waited for me to get back to the farm. But I had to be in school. I wanted to be with my books, and I wanted to talk to Jencie. I went to my room for paper.

Mother felt better after she slept.

"I have to go back to school in a few days," I told her. She knew it too. "I wonder sometimes what I'm doing there," I said as we talked.

She smiled. "You have to go to school?"

"You know I do," I answered. "I belong on the farm with you, but now I have to be in Fayetteville."

Reverend Stonesifer came by to pray for Mother, and Stanley brought her a wooden goose that was a wind-gauge with whirligig wings, and nailed it to the fencepost by the mailbox. She could watch it from her window.

I knew Mother closed her ears when Reverend Stonesifer prayed. For her, the Bible all went a different way. She stuffed it with parts from other worlds. She followed a road Reverend Stonesifer couldn't recognize. *It took Jesus to stun the snake coiling around the heart,* Reverend Stonesifer said in Mother's room.

"Jesus has a snake leash," she looked at me.

STORIES THE ROCKS TELL

I had this dream there were more people in our farmhouse than Harrison and Mother and me. I dreamed it over and over. Nothing but the thinnest, somehow agreed-upon, arbitrary line between us. Nothing but definition separated animal and land and people and spirit. They interchanged like roads in Arkansas. Wounded and wounding. They moved through the farmhouse at night. Sometimes they sped by my face. Maybe the underwater people on their way to the lake. Maybe Mother's Indian people. Maybe the snakes and monkeys on the way to their dance. Often time jumped its ruts when they passed. I knew it was long ago in the night. The whole outside crowding into the farmhouse.

Ruuummph. Rumph.

That's how the rocks talked.

FAYETTEVILLE

When Jencie was gone, I spent the weekend without talking to anyone. I finished classes and work. I wrote and ate and went to bed. I put my paw in the air and felt no one. *Cedric* I whined once, and closed my eyes in the dark.

In the night, I woke with the dream of rabbits bleeding. One had its mouth run over, unable to speak. Another had a back leg dangling beneath its tail.

I WASN'T READY YET TO GO

It was all I knew. Arkansas from Bull Shoals to Haran. Even Fayetteville was on the near side of the lake. Jencie wanted me to travel with her in the summer. She talked about it as we studied, though it was still months away.

"But I've hardly been off Kingdom Road." I was studying for an exam, but she would not be quiet.

"Izzard, Yellville, Fender, Piggott, Hand." Jencie read the map of Arkansas on her desk in our room when she got restless and tired of studying. "Old Joe, Mozart, Jerusalem, Stamps. How can you not go?" she asked, knowing that I liked names. "Hogeye, Little Flock, Solgohachia, Tea Table—"

"I have to stay with Mother this summer. Besides, Jencie, I have to work." I said as I heard the winter storm against our window. "I don't want Harrison selling another hog for tuition. He can hardly pay taxes as it is. And Bently wants me at the backwoods with him." Harrison wrote that I could also work at Hathcoat's. Another store in that small lake town! He finished his letter.

YOU SAW MY POEMS IN THE *HARAN NEWS*?

"I did." Bently was at the farmhouse when I returned from Fayetteville for Nasha's late winter wedding.

"Whad you think of them?"

"I didn't know what to think. My wife and I read them at supper."

"I guess poetry is like skipping a stone on the edge of the lake and telling only the places it hit, without the water spaces between the thud and splats." I paused.

"Words thrown into the air."

"Possibly," I said to Bently.

I saw him smile at me. "It's the unfolding of everything that feels folded. It's benevolent hands reaching out to you?"

"Yes," I answered.

"Your poems are a little like some of Stanley's inventions."

SHIVAREE

Stiff blades of grass shimmied at the edge of the church house. Nathan and his wife, Dempster, Wylie, and I shivered in the truck near the grove of fir trees, waiting for Nasha and her husband to come from the church after they were married.

They would live in Haran, had rented a small house with a narrow closet, where McElhanney already had his jacket, a pair of boots, and several pair of jeans. Later they wanted to move to Fort Smith.

Soon Reverend Stonesifer, the Pierce brothers and their wives left the church. Then Nasha and her husband, helping her into his truck in the cold wind. After they passed, we followed them down Kingdom Road with our kettle-lids for the shivaree.

FORT SMITH

The summer after Nasha's wedding, I worked in Fort Smith for tuition. Reverend Stonesifer's wife had a cousin, Mrs. Pradmore, who had a rooming house where I stayed. I worked during the day and wrote at night before I slept.

"Do you know I woke up one night after I'd gone to sleep and heard you scratching in your room like a hen," Mrs. Pradmore said. "What do you do in there all by yourself?"

"I keep a journal of my days in Fort Smith."

"You don't say." She handed me a letter I hoped was from Cedric, but it was Harrison's. She left her blue-checked apron on the peg.

CONTENTION

Bently had taken his wife to the market in Haran. She came in the back door of our farmhouse with squash, pumpkin, strawberry corn, black-eyed peas, corn relish, cider, and an armful of wild-flowers.

"Tarnation," Stanley said. "What do you think we grow?"

Jencie had come back to the farm with me for another visit from school. "You Pierces sure look alike," she said.

Bently's wife still stood in the door talking, thinking everyone was looking at her wares and listening to her, but she was only in the way and no one could get past.

"The deacons want Harrison to paint the church house again," Mother said when they were in the yard with Stanley and Bently, "but he isn't able. Reverend Stonesifer just don't understand we get old."

"It can't go much longer," Harrison said, "with heat and cold beating against it, wind, rain and sleet." The sun had fingers always picking at the paint on the boards. "And no one wants to paint it."

The hired man's boy came to the porch and Jencie and I talked to him for a while. Soon the hired man called Rupert, and he left. Mother asked him to stay but he said that he had to be going.

"Cedric and Ann have come for a visit," I heard Bently's wife say in the backyard, and looked at Mother. In the Arkansas autumn, the leaves turned yellow, rust, applewine, orange and maroon. I saw Harrison shuffle across the farmyard to the barnlot with Stanley to look at Jude, who was ailing.

My legs quivered.

"I didn't know," Mother said to me. "I heard her say that Cedric had come when you and Jencie were on the front steps talking to Rupert."

"Cedric and Ann are with us for several days," Bently said as he walked up behind me.

As I turned to go into the farmhouse, and Bently's wife took her wares to the car, I saw Cedric turn into our drive from Kingdom Road. I knew who it was before I could see them in the car and it was too late to run.

I stood stiffly in the drive of our farmhouse while they drove up. I bit my lip.

"I told Ann you'd be at Harrison's or Stanley's," Cedric said to his mother.

"You went off and left us for the morning," Ann said.

"We thought we'd leave you with some time to yourselves," Bently's wife said, putting the last basket of strawberry corn in Bently's car.

"That's why we came—" Ann told her, "to visit with you. We have time to ourselves at home."

Stanley's family had passed on their way to Haran and were still at the farm too. Everyone had come that Saturday but Nasha and her husband, and Dempster and Wylie, who had taken Bently's truck to Haran, where Dempster had a girl.

"Jean." Bently's wife said and held out her hand to me. "This is Ann."

"'lo," I said. She stood with Cedric in the leaves that blew down upon us in the wind. "Cedric." I spoke to him.

I hurried into the farmhouse as Bently's wife had Ann meet Nathan's wife and Jencie. I sobbed a while in the kitchen and dried my face when Mother came into the house with some of the strawberry corn Bently's wife had decided to give her. Soon I returned to the yard, though I knew my eyes were red.

"It was the extreme of heat and cold," Stanley was agreeing about the church house. I heard him say that houses didn't last long in America. He had been in Europe during the war where houses lasted two hundred years and more. "In America," Stanley said, "the buildings are old at fifty."

"A hundred degrees in summer. Eighteen in winter. Year after year," Harrison said. "What can you expect?"

I looked at Cedric and Ann standing in the yard together. Eban had stayed in Missouri. He had a business with Cedric's wife, Ann Halpin-Pierce. Eban had quit the university after a year, to Bently's chagrin, and started a small clothing business with Cedric's wife. Bently called him Purdam.

Cedric had a wife, he taught at the university, and he had been published in the *Missouri Review*. I had been published in the *Haran News*.

Cedric commented on that.

He was condescending, I thought. "I wait," I stammered, "and turn up the steps to Bently's shed," my voice wobbled, "—in case a black snake's there."

Cedric laughed and I longed for him to be gone from our farm.

Nathan's child had been sick and it whimpered in the arms of Stanley's wife. Reverend Stonesifer had prayed for him at the church house.

"Sometimes we claim healing," Stanley's wife said, "and take up our bed and walk. Other times our prayers take time to be answered."

Cedric interrupted her conversation with something.

"Chut!" Bently interjected and I saw Cedric stiffen. "The Bible is the sum of conversation—our Summum Bonum," he predicated.

Ann put her hand on Bently's arm. "Now Dad," she said to him.

"This is Pierce land you're on!" he answered her.

Everyone was suddenly quiet as Ann looked at Bently, and Bently's wife was trying to quiet him.

"We don't have to take your abuse," Cedric said.

Ann took her hand from Bently's arm.

"Our heritage stepped on—trod down—" Bently was in another pother about religion.

"I have not!" Cedric shouted and Jencie looked at me.

"Not coming back here to get married—what in God's name—?"

Bently's wife didn't know what to do. "Hush, Cedric," she said before he could say anything. "Be quiet, Bently," she pleaded but they still argued as they always had.

Nathan's baby cried and Stanley took his family to their station wagon. "Bently—" Stanley's wife fluttered as they left.

Mother had her ears covered.

Harrison tried to quiet Bently as he threw some of the wildflowers at Cedric.

The church house beat with rain and heat.

Cedric and Ann got in their car and drove back up Kingdom Road with a squeal of their tires.

The hired man and his wife stood in the yard by the pump. Gerz meebo. I heard their boy in the shed.

They disgusted me—Cedric as much as Bently. I had our faith and would hold on to it. Not with Bently's tenacity but with civility, I would paint the church house.

DRIVING TO COTTER WHERE HARRISON'S TRUCK
BROKE DOWN

What fence and row of hedgetrees grew together and never made contact? Like Iscariot and the sun. The wax wings of our marriage, Cedric, are more like the old wagon wheel and the road it traveled long ago. Now both road and wagon are gone and the only wheel left makes its way to the creek like a line of cows. Smoke rises over the road ahead as I drive to get Harrison. There might be fire that would melt the wings I wear, but I don't do anything anymore except kept the car on the old road.

WINTER

And 'is hands frozen last winter on the marnin cold and parple fingers like the arse in the window box.

Kivvers hangin' on the parch rail wan doose but flapur in stiff 'ar, trubbin hoe, reap hook, harnge, choppin' ax.

Quilled the noise of tongues ifin he don't fall in the culbert 'gin, har says. They'll be unstiffuned by arternoon, f' charch anywise, te deum, day at'ter marrow.

SKETCHES OF THE ARTIST AS A WOMAN

I was at the lake on a semester break my last year of school. Patches of ice floated in the cove, and the snow was heavy on the lake woods.

I put on my woolen cap, my snow boots, and my coat, and went out the door of our cabin. As I pulled the door closed behind me, a handful of snow fell from the roof, dusting my head and coat. I brushed it from my cap and the back of my coat, and got the mittens from my pocket.

I had come to Bull Shoals early in the spring of 1946, a child still in our album under a plaid coat of my cousin's, and a muffler and galoshes that were probably Nathan's too, or Cedric's. "Jean Pierce" was written in pencil underneath. Harrison had bought the point about the lake as speculation before the dam was made. Then he built our cabin from Stanley's severence after the war, and from the property he divided from the point which he sold to Bently, who built his cabin from his teaching salary.

The snow on my collar had turned to spots of water, and I felt them run down the neck of my sweater as I tramped past the three tall trees and up the last of the hill to the lake road. The snow was quiet but for the squeak of my boots on the road and a woodpecker noise somewhere on the next hill. I could almost hear the traffic in the small lake town, which this time of year would be hunters and the student from the University of Arkansas I'd ridden with.

I took my hand from a mitten and dried the back of my neck. My breath steamed before me as I walked past the other cabins. I got a hurt in my throat when I thought of Cedric. The chill on the back of my neck from the snow came through to my throat. I was afraid of tears. They would sting in the cold against my face. I bit my lip to think of something else. I had wanted to be Cedric's wife. We were cousins, but I loved him as a husband. The narrow Osage ran into the lake, but the lake, once past the dam, became a river again.

I wiped my nose with a cold mitten. That woodpecker noise was our dock that rocked in the patches of ice. Sister Whatley's quilt against a steel thimble of barrels underneath the dock.

I walked down the same lake road that Cedric and I had walked down in the summer. But now on the narrow side of those years, I grabbed a small branch in the snow at the edge of the lake road like I used to, and pulled it behind me.

Cedric, I thought. The branch made crooked marks on the lake road, which would have been deep with tire ruts, but for the road-grader that smoothed it every summer. And when dust from the cars on the lake road reached the sky, and they could see it from the lake town, the truck with gravel would come.

If I listened harder, I could probably even hear the traffic on Interstate 40 where cars and trucks traveled through the wet highway slush. *Snain.* Bently used to say. I made jagged marks over the lake road as sketches of an artist.

I had kept journals and stored conversations with Bently. Then words came from my own shelves.

Sometimes I speak from underwater. Tons of it cover me. I will never see the air. Glub—I open my mouth. I will work all my life toward the long way out. I will come up with the light.

I hurried down the lake road for a walk to get out of the cabin for a while. I thought about Cedric far away in Missouri. I was the barrel-rim of his ribs—I walked to the edge of the lake road and lay down on the snow bank, looking at the sky. *He was older than me,* he told me. I saw him as a father. Hadn't Harrison always been in the creekbottoms? But Cedric wasn't a father to me. *We're cousins, Jean. I've known cousins who married,* I answered.

I walked on the road again, leaving my branch. A small rush of snow fell from the branches where I passed, hitting the ground with a thud, the way the dust would fly from the lake road under our running feet. Sister Whatley had shaken her quilt, still at work, as she ripped a crooked patch and straightened it on her lap, spilling the threads of her snow.

The noise of a fishing boat far out on the lake sounded like Stanley's plane the one time he got it off the field on his farm. But he couldn't go far. Not much past what Jude and Grace could have walked.

So many years Nate, Eban, Dempster, and I had rowed our old wooden rowboat around the lake. But the *Commodore* had rotted with termites, and her hull was now the crescent moon coming up on the horizon.

The lake had been ours under the splintered oars of the *Commodore*, but no longer. The Ozark country had changed. Even the backwoodsmen at Salmer's Landing had finally disappeared into the woods.

Now the lake was crowded with boats, and in those boats, people who didn't understand the lake. There were only a few places where the lake was still in its wilderness, on our point and in the backwoods of my remembering.

Snow was heavy on the lake woods where there was a trail of chimney smoke like a ladder between our lake woods and the woods out beyond the stars, where a cranky God crept up and down at night, tossing us this way or that, condemning us in our fallen state, yet licking us with his tongue as we worked our way through the animal kingdom of Arkansas. Not able to speak or know the reality of things, but making facsimiles with our words.

"We was supposed to be our different ways." Sometimes I could hear Mother's voice. "Before the Tower of Babel we was all alike. Then we was separated. For our own good." She'd look straight at Bently. "So we wouldn't go so far together we couldn't get back."

"With tongues we were separated. With the tongues God gave us in church, we are brought together." Bently summed, agreeing with Mother for once.

As I walked on the snowy lake road, sometimes I thought I could see God crouched above the dark trees. Someday I would plow my fingers into the fields of his life.

Far away I could hear the traffic. Maybe even Interstate 40 between Fort Smith and Little Rock where the trucks traveled through the frozen slush, trailing wet steamers like the schoolyard Maypole.

I WALKED DOWN THE LAKE ROAD WITH DEMPSTER

"Where are we going?" he asked.

"On a walk."

"How far will we go?" the porker said.

"We will walk until your mother lets you back in the cabin."

He threw a rock down the hill toward the lake. I saw Nate and Eban fishing from the *Commodore*.

"What will we do?"

"We'll just walk, Dempster," I said. "We could look for my cove. Or we could look for the monkey kingdom in Arkansas."

"Where is it?"

"I don't know." I was irritated with Dempster.

He kicked the mound of dirt and gravel left by the road grader along the sides of the road.

"I don't want to go into the woods."

"Don't worry," I told him. "I don't either."

Dempster called to Nate and Eban, but they didn't answer. I saw the vines in the trees above us. Old trapezes the monkeys made to *evilate* the world. Dempster was hitting the weeds with a stick and I walked down the lake road until Dempster was far behind.

AH! THE STIRRING OF THE SUPPER KETTLE

Leaves, words, ankle-bone, thigh.

I had the idea of faith, which I heard in church, and the image of my cove in the sky. They fused in the supper kettle.

I felt it in the boat in summer.

Cedric would be angered at my thoughts, and his anger would show like the unsightly shore when the lake was low.

I went over my concepts again like Bently's wife had gone over the boys for wood ticks.

I was alone as I worked, yet I had everyone around me. I heard their voices in my words.

I stood over the supper kettle and stirred the greens, onions, and redeye gravy.

IT CAME AND WENT LIKE WAVES ON THE LAKE

Nasha and I looked in the window at Cedric flat in the bed they moved into the kitchen.

"In his fever, they have to keep him warm?" Nasha asked.

"The faith of our Mother and Father Pierce, and those gone before them, would preserve Cedric's life." Bently kept a vigil. It was a standard set for our lives. The fever could come so far, and no farther.

Bently's wife, pregnant with her fourth child, hovered over them. I felt the white seeds I got at my mother's.

The churchwomen prayed. Sister Whatley sat looking at everyone in Bently's wife's kitchen. "Glory to God," she said. Her hair blowing as if from the whiz of Stanley's wind gauges all over our farms.

Nasha and I felt the *thwak* of the fever-spirits trying to get out. *Whack whack* they hit the kitchen window with little sputs. Nasha screamed, and even I ducked when they hit like pebbles Ratsy threw at us at school.

They hit the windows like the spirits I heard my mother say flew from her mother when she died. Us traveling all the way back by bus, by wagon, to her farmhouse. The pigs squalling. The land wiping its runny nose.

CEDRIC CALLED US UNDER THE DOCK

My feet looked far away when I put them down, but I held them against my life jacket, waiting for the fish to gather under our dock, watching their blue that looked green in the water gather slowly beneath us until we yelled and they darted away.